What the critics are saying…

"…is a recommended read and a keeper to pull out and re-read each year in February." ~ *Claudia McRay Romance Junkies*

"*Candy Store* is an absolutely amazing story. Delectable and rich, Callie and Tobey light up the pages with their passion… *Ms. Andre* is a talented writer and I look forward to reading more of her work." ~ *Sharyn McGinty, In the Library Reviews*

"The characters were well developed for short stories and the storylines were easy to follow. It goes without saying the sexual scenes were pulsating hot. It is what readers of Ellora's Cave books come to expect and they get their money's worth in this anthology… If you are looking for something special to honor Valentine's Day, this up your alley." ~ *Susan, Fallen Angel Reviews*

```
Paperback Trade Inn
145 East Fourteen Mile Rd
Clawson, MI 48017
' (248) 307-0226
```

"*Candy Store* is a fun, creative and sizzling story. The love scenes are incredibly hot and original. You'll be craving more than chocolate after reading it. ...well-written tales, full of love, romance and hot, steamy sex." ~ *Renee, Sizzling Romances*

5 stars "Bella Andre's Candy Store is the first treat in this excellent Valentine's anthology. ...*Candy Store* is a novella filled with lust and passion and sex scenes to match..." ~ *JERR –Mireya Orsini*

Sweet TREATS

Mlyn Hurn
Bella Andre

ELLORA'S CAVE
ROMANTICA PUBLISHING

An Ellora's Cave Romantica Publication

www.ellorascave.com

Sweet Treats

ISBN #1419952838
ALL RIGHTS RESERVED.
Candy Store Copyright © 2003 Bella Andre
Valentine Wishes Copyright © 2003 Mlyn Hurn

Candy Store Edited by Raelene Gorlinsky
Cover art by: Syneca

Trade paperback Publication: November, 2005

Excerpt from *Shooting Stars* Copyright © Bella Andre, 2004

With the exception of quotes used in reviews, this book may not be reproduced or used in whole or in part by any means existing without written permission from the publisher, Ellora's Cave Publishing, Inc.® 1056 Home Avenue, Akron OH 44310-3502.

This book is a work of fiction and any resemblance to persons, living or dead, or places, events or locales is purely coincidental. The characters are productions of the authors' imagination and used fictitiously.

Warning:

The following material contains graphic sexual content meant for mature readers. *Sweet Treats* has been rated *E-rotic* by a minimum of three independent reviewers.

Ellora's Cave Publishing offers three levels of Romantica™ reading entertainment: S (S-ensuous), E (E-rotic), and X (X-treme).

S-*ensuous* love scenes are explicit and leave nothing to the imagination.

E-*rotic* love scenes are explicit, leave nothing to the imagination, and are high in volume per the overall word count. In addition, some E-rated titles might contain fantasy material that some readers find objectionable, such as bondage, submission, same sex encounters, forced seductions, etc. E-rated titles are the most graphic titles we carry; it is common, for instance, for an author to use words such as "fucking", "cock", "pussy", etc., within their work of literature.

X-*treme* titles differ from E-rated titles only in plot premise and storyline execution. Unlike E-rated titles, stories designated with the letter X tend to contain controversial subject matter not for the faint of heart.

Contents

Candy Store
Bella Andre
~11~

Valentine Wishes
Mlyn Hurn
~107~

Candy Store

Bella Andre

Chapter One

The orgasmic moans coming from behind Callie were too loud and impassioned for her to ignore any longer.

"Ooohh, I just died and went to heaven," exclaimed a middle-aged woman as she popped another truffle into her mouth. The teenager next to her said, "Stop hogging them all, mom," and reached across her mother to grab several treats off the tray the waiter was holding.

Callie smiled, pleased that everyone was enjoying the truffles so much, but then her smile turned into a frown as she remembered her accountant's words. *Your business better start picking up, and fast, or you're going to have to shut down Callie's Candies.* Callie slumped down in her seat with a loud sigh. Her store wasn't bringing in enough money to stay afloat. Even though everyone who had ever tasted one of her confections seemed to love them, Callie still wasn't able to make ends meet. Her accountant had arranged for her to meet with a renowned candy company consultant on Monday, but right now Callie wasn't feeling particularly hopeful about it. As soon as anyone started talking about marketing and promotion, Callie always started daydreaming about new candy creations, no matter how hard she tried to stay focused on business plans.

She looked around the indoor garden at the two hundred people who were munching on her truffles with looks of utter rapture on their faces and had to blink quickly to fight back a sudden onslaught of tears. How could she give up on Callie's Candies? Making people happy was worth so much more to her than making money, she thought as she sniffled and opened her little beaded purse to look for a tissue.

The woman behind her licked bittersweet chocolate dust off of her fingers. "Wait a minute, honey. I've got a tissue here in my purse for you. I always cry at weddings myself. Everything about them is so perfect and beautiful, isn't it?"

Callie forced herself to nod and then accepted the tissue from the woman. Ignoring the chocolate smear across it from the woman's fingers, Callie blew her nose.

She liked weddings. Really she did. Especially since the happy couple had met in her store last Valentine's Day.

Callie tucked the used tissue into her purse, trying hard to clear her mind. Right now she didn't want to think about Valentine's Day. She didn't want to think about weddings. And she sure as heck didn't want to think about love.

She snorted at the thought of love—didn't one need a boyfriend or even, say, a date first?—and the woman next to her scooted a little farther away. Callie felt tears well up in her eyes again. Even a middle-aged stranger thought she was weird and wanted to get away from her. Callie reached for the used tissue and blew again.

The first few chords of the wedding march rang out and the guests leapt to their feet. Callie noted that everyone was either still chewing and swallowing or licking chocolate off of their fingers as they waited for the bride to appear. She bit back a slightly hysterical laugh.

At least there is one thing about me that people love, she thought as the radiant bride appeared from an arbor of white lattice and pink roses.

Too bad she couldn't barter chocolate truffles for love.

* * * * *

Tobey stood next to the priest and tried not to sway. Planting his feet in a wide stance he clasped his hands behind his back and focused his eyes on the woman in white coming towards him.

Ruthless memories assaulted him. *What woman in her right mind would want to marry you? Candy is for children and I want a man.*

Everything blurred and Tobey had to close his eyes to keep his feet firmly planted on the ground.

The priest leaned towards him. "This is a wedding, not a wake, son."

Tobey forced a grin even though he thought his face might crack with the strain just as James, Tobey's best friend since the first grade, turned and gave him a thumb's up.

God, how he hated weddings. After his one pathetic attempt at holy matrimony, which had ended before "I do" was done, Tobey had vowed never to set foot within a mile of a wedding ever again.

And now, here he was, the best man. He knew he was a sucker, but when push came to shove he couldn't let James down. Missing his best friend's wedding would have been the coward's way out. Tobey was going to look his demons in the eye, support his friend on the happiest day of his life, and then get the fuck out.

Were it not for several quick swigs of tequila he wouldn't have made it this far. And Tobey knew damn well that several more shots would be necessaryto help him get through the reception. It was the only way.

Jane's father kissed her on the cheek and handed the bride over to the groom. Tobey saw the love flowing between them and felt nothing but emptiness inside him.

The memory tackled him again. *The Candy King? Why can't you be more like your brother?*

Tobey tried to shake the shrill voice of his faithless bitch of an ex-fiancée out of his head to focus on the ceremony that had just begun. He knew she was right, though, and that was the worst thing of all. So what if he loved what he did and was good at it? What did it matter if he was a connoisseur of candy? Who cared if he knew how to sell it, lots of it, for any company that hired him?

His skills were the skills of a child. It was time to grow up.

In a daze of self-loathing, Tobey watched James and Jane exchange rings. His best friend leaned in to kiss his new wife, but all Tobey could see was the face of his ex-fiancée, screwed up in rage at him. *You've ruined my life! I could have married someone important. Someone successful. Don't ever come near me again.* In his mind's eye Tobey could still see the shock on the faces of their guests. He could still see the hatred in Gina's eyes. But worst of all, he could see how everyone agreed with her choice.

The sound of applause pulled him from his memories and he reached out his arm to the Maid of Honor. He just needed to make it down the aisle to the bartender and then everything would be all right.

* * * * *

Callie pushed the salmon around on her plate. It was delicious, but she wasn't the least bit hungry. Her lack of appetite may have had something to do with all of the newlyweds at her table. As far as she could tell there wasn't another singleton around for miles. If she had to hear one more word about engagement rings and honeymoon trips, she was going to puke. Abruptly, she pushed her chair back and made a beeline for the bar.

A tall, broad-shouldered man stood with his back to her. Callie hadn't paid much attention to the wedding ceremony, but she couldn't help but notice the striking good looks of the best man. He had looked oddly grim throughout the ceremony, but at one point when he had grinned at the groom, it was as if the sun had come out from the clouds to pour down over everyone.

Callie cursed her unfortunate weakness for tall, dark, and handsome. Her friends liked to joke that the big brutes she always fell for were the perfect counterpart to her petite blonde curves. But it wasn't really all that funny. The truth was that if the man came with a harsh past and an emptiness in his soul, she was metal to his magnet. Which may have had something to do with her still being single, she mused unhappily. If she could only find a nice, simple, happy man—yes, short, soft, and pale would have to suffice—everything would be perfect.

Oh yeah, except for the fact that she was going to have to close her store if she didn't start making a profit.

Callie fell even deeper into her misery as she made her way past the last of the tables. The best man ran a large hand through his hair and said something in a low voice to the bartender. The sound of his voice sent goose bumps running up her bare arms.

I wonder which tall, gorgeous, svelte woman he's married to? she thought, feeling more than a tad snarky. Callie knew she was being bad, but for once she didn't care. Not only was she totally unwedded and alone, but she was about to be out of a job too. Pretty soon, instead of spending her days making candy—the one thing she loved most in the world—she was going to be sitting behind a desk in an office typing memos for some executive, or reeking of grease and saying, "Would you like onions with that?"

Callie shuddered. Coming shoulder to shoulder with Mr. Handsome and Tortured, she said to the bartender, "Give me something. Anything. Just make it strong."

She had never had more than a sip of wine before—alcohol wasn't her thing, not when she could do such amazing things with sugar and chocolate—but Callie didn't care. If there was ever a time to get drunk, it was now.

The best man, who was even more striking up close, tossed back a shot of something golden then turned to face her. "She'll have a shot of tequila," he told the bartender, all the while holding her gaze with his own. Seemingly pleased by her shock at his forward behavior, he quirked an eyebrow and added, "Make it two. With lime and salt."

Callie had never seen eyes so green. Or such a gorgeous, masculine face. She blinked and tried to tear her eyes from his, but she didn't have a chance.

"Tobey Danville," he said, his voice warm and slightly thick.

Callie's tongue darted out to lick her lips. She knew she was supposed to say her name, but she was having the darnedest time just remembering to breathe around this guy. His name seemed vaguely familiar, but her brain wasn't working well enough for her to think about anything at all.

One side of his mouth quirked up, but his semi-grin was far from being a smile. "And you are?" he asked, his tone slightly mocking, as if he was used to women losing all use of their tongues whenever he deigned to speak to them.

The bartender placed a shot glass of tequila in front of Callie and she finally pulled herself away from her trance of lust. It was long past time for her to stop acting like such an idiot. What did it matter how gorgeous this guy was? He was probably married, she was definitely single and that was that.

"Callie Moore," she said without looking at him again—god forbid she get stuck in his green eyes again— and picked up the little glass. She took a small sip of the liquid and nearly spit it out.

Suddenly angry at being the butt of some stranger's joke, she turned towards Tobey, her eyes flashing. "What is this? Are you trying to kill me?"

His laughter was so unexpected that Callie took a step back.

"I take it you've never had tequila before?" he said, his words mixing with his laughter.

Callie shook her head, not trusting herself to say anything more to this awful, albeit incredible, specimen of a man. When he laughed his eyes lit up and she thought they sparkled like the ocean, which was a ridiculous thought given that the closest she'd ever come to seeing a green-blue ocean was during a documentary about Jacques Cousteau on television.

But before she could walk away—scratch that, run away—to her car and leave to go hide in her kitchen behind her store, he leaned down so that she could feel his warm breath across her cheek and said, "Won't you let me show you how?"

His softly spoken words made shivers run all the way from the tips of Callie's breasts, which were now hard points of desire, past the vee of her legs, which was suddenly hot and aching, all the way down to the tips of her toes, which were fairly curling in her high heels. Every cell in her body was quivering in anticipation of whatever it was that Tobey wanted to show her.

"God, yes," she said in an exhale, wanting him to show her far more than how to drink the bitter beverage. Right now, as far as she was concerned, he could show her anything he wanted. Preferably naked, of course.

Callie knew she should be shocked by her wanton behavior, by her shameless thoughts, but she couldn't think straight with this man invading all of her personal space.

He slid the two glasses together and picked up a slice of lime. "First, you hold the lime between your teeth, with the flesh facing me."

Obediently, Callie opened up her mouth and let Tobey slide the small green fruit between her lips. His thumb brushed lightly over her bottom lip as he did so, and even though she knew he was touching her on purpose to tease her with his power, to show her that he already controlled her body with his own, she didn't care.

"Now tilt your neck to the side," he said as he brushed her blonde curls away from her neck. With hot, sure fingers, he lightly pushed aside the neckline of her long sleeve jersey dress to bare a small patch of skin between her neck and her collarbone.

Callie was about to burst with wanting him. All he had done was touch her mouth and the tender skin on her neck and she was about to explode into a million pieces. She was shivering, but not with cold. It was a sunny day in the first week of January in frigid upstate New York, but Callie was burning up as if it was August in Barbados.

"Good. Very good," he said in a low voice, the tips of his fingers still upon her neck.

Callie held her breath waiting for whatever came next.

"I'm going to sprinkle a little salt onto your beautiful skin," he whispered, shaking out several grains of salt onto her and Callie gasped, painfully, powerfully aware of the throbbing between her legs.

"And then," he said, in so low of a voice she could barely hear him, "it's time for the tequila."

In one smooth motion, he leaned down and sucked at the skin on her shoulder, taking the salt into his mouth. Callie groaned with pleasure as his mouth seared her with its potent heat, and then he pulled his heat away from her and downed the bitter liquid in the shot glass. Callie was so mesmerized by his every move, his every breath, she was so under his spell, that she had forgotten all about the lime between her teeth, so it was in slow motion that he leaned towards her, closer and closer, until they were finally eye to eye. With a tenderness that she could hardly believe he possessed, he placed his mouth over hers, slowly tasted her lips with his tongue, tasting every curve and the corners between her upper and bottom lips, taking his time to brand her once again before he sucked the juice from the lime.

If Callie had known that a lime could be so potent, so blatantly sexual, she would have planted a row of fruit trees in her garden long ago. She would have become a master of lemon tarts and key lime pies. Tobey removed the lime from her mouth with his teeth. Dazed, she watched him pluck it from his mouth and put it in the empty shot glass. Loud clapping for the band playing at the reception brought Callie back to reality.

Had a stranger just licked salt off of her shoulder and then sucked a lime from between her teeth?

But before she had time to fall all the way back to earth, Tobey leaned down and whispered in her ear the two words that were to be her downfall.

"Your turn."

Callie stood dumbly, unable to make any part of her body work. This gorgeous man actually thought she was going to lick salt from his neck and then suck a lime from his lips?

As if sensing her reservations, he said, "You don't want to waste your drink, now do you?"

Callie slowly shook her head. "No. It's just that I," she stuttered, unsure of what she could possible say to get herself out of this crazy predicament.

What was she doing? She was a nice girl who owned a candy store, for god's sake. Not some wanton slut who picked up men at weddings. She sneaked a glance down at his ring finger and breathed a sigh of relief. At least she wasn't a husband stealing slut. As doubts threatened to take her over, she remembered her store and how she was going to lose it. Suddenly, it was all too much for her to deal with.

"Oh, what the hell," she said. Before she could change her mind, she picked up the slice of lime and shoved it into Tobey's mouth.

Her quick action must have stunned him and pleased him all at the same time, because his eyes crinkled and he chuckled from around the lime.

Callie narrowed her eyes and looked up at him. He was going to regret laughing at her. She'd show him. She might look like a tiny blonde candy maker, but she could give as good as she got.

At least she hoped she could.

Blocking out any thoughts of where she was and how unseemly their drinking game was during the middle of a wedding reception, Callie focused on the task at hand: to make Tobey want her even more than she wanted him. She was going to set him on fire and then leave him high and dry after she took what she wanted.

Coming up on her tippy-toes, she smiled coyly and ran her forefinger over the juice dripping from the lime onto Tobey's full lower lip. "I should be gentler with you," she said, then brought her finger to her mouth and sucked the drop of juice dry.

Tobey's Adam's apple moved in his throat and Callie thought, *That's one point for my team.*

She took her finger from her mouth and brought her hands up to the bow tie of his tux. "You've got an awful lot of clothes on, don't you?"

Tobey raised an eyebrow as if to say, *So what are you going to do about it?*

Even with a slice of lime between his lips he looked daunting and powerful and far, far too sure of himself. Callie matched his silent dare with a cheeky grin. Licking her lips, with great concentration she ran her small hands down the front of his tux, from his broad shoulders, down past his well-formed pecs, to what she assumed was a washboard stomach.

Callie felt a moment of insecurity reach in to her bravado. *Think quick*, she urged herself, and right as she was wondering if she was indeed up to the task of seducing the seducer, she noticed Tobey's large, workman-like hands.

Callie took one of his lightly calloused hands in her own. She ran the tip of her finger along the soft skin and muscle at the curve between his thumb and forefinger and smiled with pleasure at Tobey's exhale of breath. Her heart beating far too fast, she slowly turned his hand over and continued tracing the skin on his palm.

More turned on than she'd ever been before — and all this in public with a man she'd known for five minutes with her clothes on and intact — Callie pushed the sleeve of his tuxedo jacket up to his forearm. Working to keep her fingers steady, trying to keep herself from simply jumping Tobey right then and there and riding him in the middle of the wedding reception, Callie undid the gold cufflink from his dress shirt and let it drop to the floor.

Neither Callie nor Tobey watched the cuff link fall to the ground. They were intent on each other, wrapped up in the escalation of their game. Slowly, precisely, Callie folded Tobey's starched sleeve up once, then twice. Every time her skin brushed against his, heat surged through her.

Tobey's pulse beat rapidly under the exposed skin of his wrist and she wanted to cover his heartbeat with the heat of her mouth.

"Perfect," she breathed, as she ran her thumb over his pulse-point. The spell remained unbroken as she reached for the salt shaker and sprinkled salt on to his tanned wrist and the edge of his palm. Raising his wrist to her mouth, Callie brought her lips to his skin and waves of desire washed through her as their bodies made contact again. She groaned as she sucked at him, hardly tasting the salt, desperate for a taste of Tobey's essence, so potent and male and wonderful. Unwilling to lose contact with him, she licked a grain of salt off of the firm flesh on his palm and she heard a low sound from his throat, like a caged lion on the verge of escape.

Knowing she needed to drink the fiery liquid, promising herself his mouth if she could tear her lips away from his wrist, Callie reached for the shot glass and drank the tequila in one long swallow. But this time it wasn't bitter and she didn't think it was going to kill her. Instead it made her feel warm, even warmer than she already was, and languid and perfect. She got back up on her tippy-toes and placed her hands behind Tobey's neck and felt softness on her fingers as she threaded them into his hair. He leaned into her and she placed her teeth around the lime and sucked the juice from it without ever touching her skin to his, and then suddenly the lime was gone and she was kissing him, and his tongue was in her mouth, conquering her, showing her that she was going to have to play the game by his rules.

Callie felt his strong hands encircle her back and pull her into him. She felt safe and hot and scared and wet and she wanted to curl up inside Tobey and never come out.

"Ahem." The bartender cleared his throat. And then again, but louder this time. "I think the bride and groom are trying to get your attention."

Callie heard the bartender from within a deep red fog, but she wanted to ignore it, if hearing him meant leaving heaven.

It was Tobey who finally pulled away from her. With one last heavy look, his devil-may-care grin was back on his face. Everything hit her at once, and Callie felt as if she had been thrown from a hot tub to a cold plunge with no warning. But it was worse than that. Everyone at the wedding had just witnessed her throwing herself at a stranger.

Knowing her thoughts, Tobey leaned in and whispered, "No one could see you behind me. There's nothing to worry about."

Callie nodded quickly as tears welled up in her eyes for the hundredth time that day. Unable to meet his eyes, she turned and ran blindly away from the gathering, instinctively heading for the one place that she would feel safe again—the kitchen.

She darted through the swinging door and stepped to the left just in time to avoid a collision with one of the waiters. Her eyes wild, she ran past the prep area, past the stoves, rounded a corner and found refuge in the walk-in refrigerator. Stepping inside, she slumped down onto an upside down milk crate and tried to catch her breath.

She was just going to have to hide in the refrigerator until the reception was over. It was either that or risk running into Tobey again. Which she definitely couldn't do. One more minute so near to him, and she'd be naked and riding him for sure.

Chapter Two

"May the bride and groom have true love forever!"

Tobey raised his champagne glass in a toast to James and Jane, doing his best to act the part of the happy best man, but all he could think about was the little blonde vixen who had just run away from him.

"Has anyone seen Callie?" Jane asked after the endless toasts were through. At her guest's blank stares, she added, "She made the incredible truffles."

People moaned with remembered pleasure and licked their lips and said things like, "Better than sex," and "Are there more?"

Tobey smiled. He should have known that Callie had something to do with candy. Candy was, after all, his specialty. And Callie was so damn sweet, especially her plump lips and the succulent patch of skin at the base of her neck. He couldn't wait to taste the rest of her. He was going to run his tongue over every inch of her body, from her lush breasts and her taut nipples, which he was guessing were a dusty rose on the light creamy skin of her breasts, to the valley between her thighs, and…

Jane's voice cut through his X-rated daydream. "Darn. I wish she was here so I could officially thank her for making those incredible truffles that everyone has been raving about." Jane reached for her new husband's hand. "Plus, if it weren't for Callie's Candies, James and I would have never found each other."

James leaned over and frenched his newly wedded wife. Tobey shifted from one foot to the other in discomfort and looked away. *Get a room*, he thought, but then, he and Callie had practically been humping at the bar, so who was he to complain?

When his best friend was finally done kissing his bride, he turned towards Tobey with a knowing grin. "Any idea where Callie might be?"

"Not a clue," Tobey answered truthfully. "But I'd be happy to go find her for you."

"I bet you would," James said with a wink. "For us."

Finally free of his best man duties, Tobey headed for the door that Callie had run through. He hoped that she hadn't left the reception altogether. They had some unfinished business to take care of. Preferably while they were naked in a room with a lock.

"The kitchen," he said to himself, when he walked into the large cooking area. "That makes sense."

"Did anyone see a small blonde woman run through here?"

One of the waiters nodded towards the hall behind the prep area and the stoves. "She went back there."

Tobey nodded his thanks. Once he had walked around the corner into the hidden, back area of the kitchen, he saw two large doors, both big enough for him to step through. Opening the door to his right, he realized it was a commercial freezer, packed full of ice cream containers and huge bags of ice.

He closed the heavy freezer door and turned his gaze to the refrigerator door, a broad grin taking over his face. He almost felt sorry for his hot little candy maker.

She may have intended on cooling off in the fridge, but he was going to make sure that she got hot, hot, hot instead.

* * * * *

Callie heard a noise in the hall and looked up through the thick, frosted glass on the refrigerator door. "Shit," she whispered. A tall man in a tux was standing just outside the door. It had to be Tobey. She tried to push herself back further into the shelves, hoping that her dark pink dress would help her to blend in with the crates of supplies. Maybe if she didn't move, didn't make a sound, didn't even breathe, he would go away. And she could be left in peace with her memory of the taste of his skin and the beating of his heart on her lips.

Callie had spent the past ten minutes rubbing the goose bumps on her arms and trying to convince herself that she had had enough of Tobey. She had firmly decided that she was going to be perfectly happy masturbating in the shower to the sexy picture of Tobey that she had fixed in her mind's eye. She didn't need to see him, didn't need to touch him, didn't need any more of his kisses.

But now that he was standing only feet from her—somehow she had known all along that he would find her and now he had—it was all she could do not to fling the door open, pull him inside the cramped 5'x5' space with her, and rip all of his clothes from his body.

Who was she kidding? She wasn't going to be content with just the memory of him, with just her dreams of what it would be like to feel him naked against her, writhing in pleasure.

At the same time, an annoying inner voice of reason was telling Callie that there was no use in giving in to her baser needs. One night of mind-blowing sex wasn't going to help anything. It wasn't going to save her business. It wasn't going to save her pathetic love life.

Although, she thought with a grin, it was guaranteed to be fun.

The doorknob turned and Callie gasped. He was coming in. What was she going to do? She stood up and backed into the wall, pressing herself up against the cold edge of the laden shelves as hard as she could.

In the dim light of the refrigerator, Tobey's warm voice wrapped around her. "I thought I might find you in here."

Callie was both alarmed and aroused by his presence, by the way he filled up the room with his essence. The crazy mix of feelings made it hard for her to speak.

"I, uh…" she said as she watched Tobey open the door and step into the refrigerator with her, his eyes drinking hungrily of her, noting her taut, cold nipples through the thin silk of her bra, noting the way she had pressed herself up against the shelves to try and hide from him. She was sure that he could read the need in her eyes, even as she tried to hide it from him.

Less than four feet from her, which was at least four feet too close for Callie's comfort, Tobey closed the door behind him with a soft but definite click, never once taking his eyes from her.

His voice laced with humor, he said, "There's no lock, but at least it's private. We'll just have to hope no one needs any milk."

Looking for a way out, for some sort of escape path, willing herself to think fast so that she could get the heck away from him, she said, "Actually, I was looking for the milk, for, um, coffee for the reception." Picking up a carton of milk, she said, "So now that I've found it, I…"

Tobey took a step towards her and Callie, who felt as if she was the lioness being hunted by a needy lion, dropped the carton of milk on the floor. It broke open and splashed onto her shoes, but she hardly noticed.

All she could feel was his heat. She knew he could feel hers, as if she was drawing him to her via some sort of sexual infrared. No matter how many times she told herself she didn't want what he was offering her, no matter how she tried to convince herself that she didn't need the release that he promised her, she knew that she did.

Desperately.

Tobey pinned her against the shelves with one arm on either side of her. "You weren't looking for milk," he said, his voice husky. "You were looking for this."

He leaned in and captured her mouth in a kiss so sweet, so powerful, that Callie was instantly infused with a deep warmth. But even as her passion grew, Callie worried. "What if someone walks in?"

Tobey laughed off her fears, unconcerned. He nipped at her lips, biting softly at the incredibly sensitive, cool flesh, burning her up. Vaguely noting that her skirt was hiked all the way up around her waist, Callie thought, *Thank god I'm not wearing nylons*. Tobey's fingers made their way up the soft flesh of her inner thigh, teasing her with their intent. He hiked one of her legs up against his thigh and, breathless with anticipation, Callie felt herself grow more and more swollen, until finally he pushed past the wispy silk of her panties and found her slick and ready and wet.

He pushed his palm against her inflamed mons and Callie pushed her weight into his hand, no more able to stop herself from grinding into him than she would have been able to walk away and leave him.

All the while, even as her breath caught, even as the hard flesh of his palm aroused her clitoris until she almost hurt with it, Tobey was driving her crazy with his gentle kisses.

Until now, Callie had always been perfectly happy to let the man lead in bed. She had been content to let her lovers take their time exploring her, to even show them how she liked to be touched for even greater pleasure.

But now, in this moment, Callie knew that if she didn't get more of Tobey—his mouth, his hands, the huge, hard shaft that was pressing against his black tuxedo pants and now against her palm as she cupped his heavy weight—she was going to die. She plunged her tongue into his mouth and found his, forcing it to mate with hers. She heard him make a sound of pleasure, she thought she matched his moan with her own, but she didn't care. She didn't care about anything other than mating with this glorious man, whose touch turned her skin to flames.

Lifting his mouth from hers, Tobey reached for the jersey fabric of her dress. "I need to see you," he said in a low voice.

Callie pulled her dress up over her head then reached for Tobey's jacket, roughly yanking it off of his shoulders. "I need to taste you," she said as she ripped off his bow tie and jerked his shirt open at the neck.

Her lips and tongue found the hollow of his neck, found his strong, quick pulse, and with every moment she grew wetter and readier for Tobey than she had ever been for any man.

He slid his hands to her back, stroking flames onto her skin, and then her bra was on the floor, and his sure fingers overtook hers, clumsy with cold and need as she tried to remove his shirt. Knocking off several cartons of milk from a low shelf beside them, he propped her up on it. Callie reached for his belt, but he had already dropped to his knees, his mouth at her breasts, licking and sucking at the soft, plump flesh, coming closer and closer to her nipples, but not nearly close enough.

Already puckered from the refrigeration, her areolas tightened into tiny buds of bliss as he licked slow circles around them, almost flicking against her nipples, but never quite touching them.

"Please," Callie moaned, her hands wound into Tobey's thick, dark hair, her head thrown back, her back arched. She pushed her tits into him, any remaining vestiges of modesty gone, impatient for him to put her out of this exquisite agony.

"Not yet," he said, taking her ample breasts into his hands. Reverently, he ran his thumbs lightly over her nipples, then back again, flicking the tight buds with his fingers.

"Dusty rose. I knew it," he said softly as he worshiped her. His mouth consumed her as he tasted every square inch of her glorious breasts, rising up from her rib cage to the taut peak of her nipples. "You're so beautiful. So damn beautiful."

Callie had always been more than a little embarrassed by the size of her breasts—D cups on a five foot frame had always seemed way out of proportion—but if Tobey continued to lick and suck her like that, she vowed to never have another bad thought about them again.

"Oh god, yes," she whimpered, her sounds of pleasure muffled by the thick walls of the refrigerator.

She was so hot, burning up everywhere he touched her. And then his hands were lifting her up and pulling her panties off of her, the wispy silk scratching the sensitive skin on her inner thighs. Her panties fell to her ankles and she kicked them off, along with her shoes. And then Tobey's head was between her legs, his tongue on her.

He lightly touched the tip of her clit, engorged and so sensitive. Instinctively, Callie opened her legs up wider and bucked her hips up into his mouth.

Callie knew he was intent on teasing her because he held her firmly away from his mouth, lapping at her once, then twice, then blowing lightly on her heated flesh.

"More," she cried, no longer worried about anyone walking in on them, no longer caring if anyone in the kitchen heard her scream out for him.

A smile on his lips, he reached for her and brought her lips to his, letting her taste her juices, letting her lick them from his tongue.

"You have the sweetest pussy," he said, and she said, "Please."

His hand on her thigh, only inches from her lips, he said, "Tell me what you want."

Callie didn't even have to think. "Lick me."

Tobey licked her kneecap. "Here?" he asked, his eyes devious and challenging.

"No," she cried, wishing he would give her what she wanted, wishing she didn't have to say the words.

He licked the tender flesh on the inside of her elbow. "Here?"

Callie gave in. "My pussy," she whispered, amazed to hear the word roll off her tongue. "Lick my pussy," she said again, her voice louder, more sure as she realized how much she liked the feel of the word as it rolled from her tongue to her lips and then out into the cold air of their private refrigerated world.

Tobey kissed her hard on her lips, bruising them, before kissing a trail down her flesh, from the hollow of her neck to the valley between her lush breasts.

"I," he pulled at her nipples with his mouth, causing shivers of ecstasy to race down Callie's spine, "would be happy," his tongue dipped into her belly button, "to lick," and then lower still to the very tip of her clit, "your pussy."

In an instant his mouth was on her, hot and insistent. His tongue plunged in and out of her canal, he sucked on her swollen clit, and Callie cried out as all of the pressure that had been building up since she first saw Tobey standing at the bar threatened to explode into a million glorious pieces. Impossible tremors wracked her, knocking her back against the shelves, pushing her off the counter into Tobey's lips and teeth and hands. He slipped a finger into her slick, pulsing canal, then two. Callie felt her muscles clench around him, trying to take his thick fingers even deeper and she envisioned his cock pumping in and out of her, just like his fingers were doing, rough and powerful and perfect. Her heart pounding so hard, faster than she thought it could, the rainbow of colors faded away, and Callie fell limp in Tobey's arms.

* * * * *

Still on his knees, sticky in a pool of milk, Tobey could hardly think. He could hardly breathe. He was no stranger to sweaty, grinding sex, but he couldn't help but be amazed by what happened to him with this woman. He got within five feet of her and he lost his mind. He had to have her. Every perfect inch of her.

He grinned as he felt the last of her contractions press down on his fingers. He was pleased, more pleased than he could ever say, that Callie obviously felt exactly the same way about him. He had always had a thing for stacked little blondes, but this one was putting every other woman he'd been with to shame. She was heedless in her passion, shy yet demanding, hungry, yet waiting for him to make the next move.

His grin fell away. His cock throbbed in his pants, demanding attention. Tobey hadn't been this hard since he was sixteen, about to stick his dick into his first pussy. He didn't think he could hold off much longer.

With his free hand, he undid his belt buckle and unzipped his pants, then reached for the condom in his back pocket. Steadying Callie, who had leaned her weight against him as she recovered from the huge orgasm that had ripped through her, Tobey slowly slid his fingers from her, pressing one last kiss to her sweet cunt, licking her sweet juices off of his lips before he rose up from his knees.

Finally, the tip of his cock rested at the incredibly wet, pink entrance to her vagina, his hugely swollen head red with insistence. Tobey wanted to plunge into her, roughly, forcefully, until he exploded. He wanted to overpower her, to squeeze her enormous breasts, to feel them heavy in his hands as he rode her, dominated her. He wanted to grab her ankles and push them over her shoulders, opening up her thighs wide so that he could watch his cock sink into her, inch by inch.

But even though he wanted to do all of this and more, he didn't. Because even more than Tobey wanted to take Callie for his own pleasure, he wanted to please her all over again. He wanted to hear her cries of ecstasy and watch her as she came beneath him.

He slipped the condom on in one smooth move, and smiled into her beautiful blue eyes. She looked up at him, shy again, and Tobey opened his mouth to murmur something comforting to her, to let her know that she was safe with him, that he was going to take his time, even if it killed him.

And then her eyes changed, turning from a clear ocean to a swirling, deep dark blue. Before he knew what had even happened, Callie had bucked her hips into him and swallowed his cock. All of it.

"Callie," he groaned against her lips. She shut him up with a kiss so full of ownership, Tobey knew right then and there that he would be hers forever.

Bucking and rearing, Tobey slid in and out of her, delirious with pleasure. Her breasts struck his chest with every thrust and Callie's kisses sucked all of the breath from him. Barely coherent, Tobey felt her muscles begin to tighten around his shaft.

Mustering what little control he had left, he held her ass still with his big hands. "Look at me."

As if from a dream, Callie opened her eyes slowly. Hazy with passion, she watched him watch her.

Tobey slid out one inch, and then another. Callie's eyelids fell shut and so he stilled again.

"Open your eyes," he said, his voice shaking with need even as he gave her his command.

Slowly she re-opened them and he thought he saw defiance in their depths.

He was right. "They're open," she whispered. "Now show me a good time."

Tobey would have laughed if he could have. Instead he thrust his cock into her pussy again and again, watching her eyes change again from a deep blue to a dark purple. As Callie's orgasm overtook her, Tobey closed his eyes, threw his head back, and came hard and long. It seemed to go on forever. He thought he would never feel so good again for the rest of his life.

But then, just as he relaxed, feeling much like he did at the end of a marathon, out of breath and exhilarated, Callie's body language changed beneath him. It might have been an imperceptible change to some men, but Tobey recognized it immediately for what it was.

Regret.

Embarrassment.

He refused to let her do it and tried to capture her mouth in a kiss, but she turned her head to the side and his lips just grazed her cheek. She wriggled her butt cheeks back into the shelves behind her and pushed at his chest. He fell out of her and she moved quickly, reaching for her bra and her dress. She threw them over her head and slipped her feet into her shoes and Tobey, figuring he'd have a better chance of reasoning with her if he had some clothes on too, quickly dressed back into his now-wrinkled, slightly milky tuxedo.

"Callie," he said. His voice was low and warm and he felt like he was trying to coax a frightened cat to drink from his bowl of milk. But he didn't get the chance to say anything else.

Loud voices sounded from the hall just as Callie put her hand on the doorknob. She turned to him. "Stay in here until everyone is gone. I'll distract them."

Tobey frowned, then nodded. He didn't want to embarrass Callie by giving away his presence, but at the same time, he couldn't let her get away.

"Wait for me," he said, but she was already out the door and gone.

Sitting down on am upside-down milk crate, Tobey rubbed his eyes with the heel of his palms. Her scent was everywhere on him.

"She's not going to get away," he promised himself as he looked around at the mess they'd made in the commercial refrigerator with a smile. "Who knew a refrigerator could be so damn hot?"

Chapter Three

The next morning, Tobey's smile could have lit up a small theatre. He planned to check in at his office, have his assistant clear his schedule, and then he was going to track down Callie Moore.

Sweet, delectable Callie Moore.

Tobey walked past the large, colorful *Sweet Returns: Candy Company Consultant* sign and into his office building in downtown Albany, New York. Alice, his assistant, looked as if she had already been hard at work for several hours. He was certain that she had been writing up invoices, balancing their accounts, keeping everything running so smoothly that all he ever had to do was think about the best ways to sell candy, even though it was just past eight in the morning.

"The king has finally arrived," she said, her mouth tight as she glanced towards the clock. Alice had managed his office since the day he'd hung out his shingle fifteen years ago and often treated him like he was no more than an unruly son who needed a ruler taken to his backside every once and again to stay on the straight and narrow. "And not a minute too soon. You need to read through several things before you meet with your new client."

Tobey sat down in a chair, guilt momentarily weighing him down. How was he ever going to let Alice go? When he closed up his candy consulting business and joined his older brother, Jed, in the accounting firm next month, he knew Alice was going to be heartbroken. Not to mention the fact that she was going to disapprove of his choice.

The smile reappeared on his face. Alice loved to disapprove of whatever it was he did. Getting her all riled up was part of the fun of working with her.

Promising himself that he'd sit down and have a talk with Alice soon, he pushed it from his mind. "I need you to clear my calendar for the day." *And hopefully for the next month or so*, Tobey thought.

He was already envisioning a trip to the Hawaiian Islands with Callie wearing nothing but a string bikini on a hot, sandy beach. He and Callie would explore their desire endlessly. Long days in the sun, followed by perfect nights under the stars. With Callie. Adorable, sensuous Callie.

Cutting into his fantasy, Alice said, "No can do. You have an important consultation today." Her voice was full of censure. Tobey wondered if she had used x-ray powers to guess his most intimate thoughts.

He was firm. "Cancel it."

Alice shook her head. "I can't and I won't. The woman I spoke to sounds sweeter than sweet, truly in love with making candy, and, most importantly, desperately in need of your help."

Tobey frowned at Alice, then got up out of the leather chair and stalked to her desk. "Fine," he said reaching his hand out for the packet of client information. "I'll go." He grabbed the file without looking at it, impatient and displeased that he wasn't going to be able to go see Callie right away. Who cared about selling candy when what waited for him was so much better than any saltwater taffy, sour ball, or chocolate bar could ever be?

"Who's the client?"

Alice surprised him with a smile. "Callie's Candies."

Tobey nearly dropped the folder. "Did you just say Callie's Candies?"

A curious glint in her eyes, Alice nodded. "That's right. My sister lives in Saratoga with that horse-crazy husband of hers and last time I went out to visit her, we dropped into Callie's Candies. Best damn truffles I ever had."

"I know," Tobey said, remembering the rapturous faces of the wedding guests as they ate Callie's truffles. They had the same look that was currently drawn across Alice's face.

"I've never seen you get so excited about candy before," he said, teasing his assistant.

"There are a lot of things you haven't seen," she snapped at him as if he were a little boy who wouldn't know up from down without her help. Returning to an all-business demeanor she said, "She's expecting you at 10 a.m. Don't be late. And don't you dare let her down."

Intent on finding out everything he could about Callie's Candies before 10 a.m., Tobey stepped into his office and closed the door. Opening the thick file of information that Alice had assembled for him, he started reading.

* * * * *

Callie's alarm went off at 7 a.m. and she burrowed down under the covers, trying to ignore it. She felt like hell today, which was no wonder, considering she hadn't slept more than fifteen minutes all night. Her dog, Wolf, got up from his big doggy bed on the floor and pushed his chin up on her pillow.

Feeling the weight of his big, shaggy head hit the bed, she emerged from beneath the down duvet. "All right, I hear you. I'm turning it off," she said. Silence descended again and Callie was certain she heard Wolf sigh with relief.

She sat up in bed, pulling the sheets up with her, and scratched Wolf's head between his ears. Just like she knew he would, he got so relaxed that his head slid off the bed and he stretched out on the rug beside her bed to go back to sleep.

The sheets scratched the tender skin of her breasts and Callie lightly ran her hands over them. Still sore and aching, they were a potent reminder of what she had done at James and Jane's wedding only a day before. All night long, images of her coming in Tobey's mouth, of his teeth grazing her shoulder as he sucked salt from her, of her thrusting into him, fucking him, desperate for him, assailed her. How could she have behaved like that? She hadn't even recognized herself in the woman she had become yesterday in his arms. Now all she wanted to do was put a closed sign on the door of her candy store and take a sleeping pill that would knock her out 'til tomorrow. She wanted to drown out her stupidity with sleep. Maybe if she slept long enough, it would all go away.

And then her life would return to normal.

Unfortunately, Callie knew that wasn't possible. Not only did she have potential customers to sell candy to—not many, of course, but the ones who came were loyal and she loved each and every one of them—but she had an important business meeting. Her accountant had set up an appointment for her with a renowned candy company consultant, Sweet something or other was the name of his company. He was going to be coming by her store at 10 a.m. this morning. No matter how bad she felt today—like a cheap, tawdry slut to tell the truth—she couldn't miss this meeting, or she'd really be screwed. Literally and figuratively.

She dragged herself out of bed, almost stepping on one of Wolf's big mutt paws. She bent over to drop a kiss on his muzzle in apology and then stepped into the shower. She turned it on full blast, praying that water could wash away some of her sins.

"I'm supposed to be the nice candy lady," she muttered, roughly soaping up her skin. "Not the truffle slut who picks up the best man and fucks his brains out."

She lathered up her arms, her legs, her stomach, trying to avoid the inside of her thighs until the last minute. She didn't want to touch herself, had held off from touching herself all night, even though her every waking moment had been filled with arousing images of her and Tobey at the bar and in the refrigerator. Her short dreams when she had fallen asleep had been even worse than that. After only a few minutes of sleep she woke up, drenched in sweat, the apex of her legs—she couldn't believe she had actually said the word pussy yesterday—throbbing with need.

But no matter how she tried, she couldn't control herself, the need Tobey unleashed in her was that great. Her hands had a mind of their own and before she knew it she was touching herself, rubbing herself, pretending that Tobey's tongue was on her again. Her clit grew huge and hard and her legs were trembling so badly that she had to lean back against the wall for support. She imagined him in the shower with her, her legs wrapped around his waist, his cock driving into her, his strong arms supporting her weight, his tongue in her mouth.

The orgasm hit her like a city bus and nearly knocked her down. She rubbed herself frantically, not wanting the tremors to end, not wanting the fantasy of Tobey being with her to be erased when she opened her eyes.

But when it was through, she shampooed her hair and dried off, utterly disgusted with herself. Forcing herself to push all erotic thoughts away, Callie dressed in her one suit, the most severe outfit she owned. The light pink suit accented her curves, the one button on the jacket showcasing her tiny waist and lush breasts and hips. Underneath the jacket, she wore a see-through silk camisole. She didn't intend to take her jacket off for the meeting—the suit was more like armor than clothes in her mind—and the white silk looked the best of anything she owned peeking out from underneath her jacket. Callie usually wore jeans and a t-shirt that said Callie's Candies on it, so today she felt business-like and stern in her suit.

She brushed her hair violently, trying to tame her unruly curls, and finally gave up. "Who am I kidding?" she said, taking one last look in the mirror. Wolf followed her out of the bedroom and she let him into the little fenced backyard to take care of his business.

"I'll come back at lunch," she called to him and he stopped sniffing the grass and turned his furry face to hers, wagging his tail as if he understood.

Sliding the screen door shut, Callie sighed. "At least somebody loves me," she said, then went to the garage to get her car. Downtown Saratoga, home to the famous horse races, was only ten minutes from her cottage. It had snowed the night before, but by 8 a.m. the streets were nicely plowed and the sidewalk slush had melted.

Callie had spent her whole life in Saratoga, but the Saratoga of today was very different from the town she knew so well as a child. Now that she might have to close her store in the near future, she took in Main Street with renewed interest.

When Callie was a little girl, she used to ride her bike into town with her friends, fifty cents in her pocket, straight to the candy store. They'd fill up their bags with jujubes and Necco wafers and jawbreakers and then head to the park and stuff themselves full of sugar under an elm tree. As a teenager, when Callie realized she had been blessed with the gift of candy making, she knew that, as soon as she could, she would open up her own candy store on Main Street.

Her dream became a reality when she was twenty-five years old. She had saved every penny from her various cooking and catering jobs over the years, only spending the bare minimum on her cottage, and all of the sweat and grease was worth it when she signed the lease for her very own candy store.

The first time she walked by the vacant storefront that was now Callie's Candies, the old rundown ice cream shop didn't look like much good for anything other than for breeding spiders and mice. Narrow but deceptively long, with a large kitchen in back, it was covered in dust and neglect.

But for Callie it was her first brush with true love. She immediately envisioned the space a buttery yellow, glass display cases full of truffles and fudge, old wine barrels on the floor with fresh, homemade saltwater taffy.

The past five years had been the most rewarding time of her life. She made candy in the evening and sold it by day. She loved watching the glee on the children's faces as they flew in off of their bikes, strewn haphazardly on the wide sidewalk, anticipation glowing in their eyes.

They knew that Miss Callie would always give them free samples of whatever she had just made that day, whether it was vanilla swirl fudge or chocolate turtle pie. And even when they pulled the dollar out of the dirty shorts and handed it to her for a bag of taffy, they couldn't wait to get outside and see what little "extra" Callie had thrown in for them, maybe a lollipop or a wax-paper-covered slice of fudge.

Sometimes, if they were really lucky, and they had been given money from their mothers for a box of truffles to take home, Callie never let them get out of the store without a handful of lollipops and gummy worms.

But now that popular chain stores ruled the street along with swanky restaurants and wine bars that seemed to multiply by the week, Callie's rent had doubled, then tripled in the past five years. With every year, she found it harder and harder to put something away in the bank after she had paid her bills. People were always telling her to put up a website and advertise, but she didn't know the first thing about that kind of stuff.

And she didn't want to. She just wanted to make candy and watch the joy on her customers' faces as they ate it.

Callie pulled into the plowed parking lot behind her building, then walked through the narrow alley between buildings to the sidewalk. She always made it a point to enter her store by the front door in the morning. Her first sight of the pretty yellow, blue, and white striped awning over the window and the fanciful cartoonish painted letters of Callie's Candies on the flag beside the door made her incredibly happy.

She unlocked the front door and walked in, pulling up the shade on the door, scanning the glass for smudges or smears. Satisfied that it was clear and clean, she headed for the back room, breathing in the scent of sugar and cocoa powder, feeling settled for the first time since the wedding the day before.

Her store didn't open until 11 a.m., Monday through Friday, but Callie always had plenty to do in the morning. The best was making fudge or coating truffles in coconut and peanuts. The worst was going through her inventory and doing her orders for the week.

Today was inventory day, of course. Callie sighed with dismay. Today of all days, she could have used a long, therapeutic session with some caramel and nougat.

"It figures," she muttered, as she walked into her small office at the back of the store and put her purse down. She took off her suit jacket and laid it across the back of her desk chair. Unbound by the jacket, her breasts felt free and immodest in the white lace camisole, reminding her yet again of her wanton behavior at the wedding.

"Forget about it. You've got work to do," she lectured herself and got straight to work, intent on ignoring the new sensual sensations her body was sending her.

Picking up her clipboard and supply spreadsheet, she went to her dry storeroom first and noted what was low. Moving to her tiny walk-in refrigerator, she checked materials off her list from the top shelf first. The bottom shelves were deep and she had to get on her knees to count cocoa bars. The position was awkward, with her rear end pointing straight up, her hands and knees sprawled unladylike on the floor. For the past five years, Callie had planned on putting in sliding shelves on the bottom of her refrigerator. Unfortunately, the project never made it to the top of her ever-growing to-do list so she hadn't gotten to it quite yet.

Squirming around, trying to get comfortable in her clumsy position, she said, "One, two, three, four," aloud as she counted stacks of the finest imported cocoa bars. Immersed in her counting and the painful crick that was building up in her neck, she was surprised by a familiar scent that suddenly overwhelmed her senses. Her inventory forgotten, she stopped counting cocoa and heard footsteps coming up the short hallway and then stopping at the doorway to her storeroom.

One thing was absolutely certain, she thought with a thudding heartbeat, she was no longer the only person in Callie's Candies.

"We've got to stop meeting in refrigerators like this."

Callie's heart stopped beating altogether. She would have recognized that smooth, deep voice anywhere. Her breasts had grown full and tight after just that one sentence. And now that she heard his voice, she knew the scent that had tipped her off was one she would never forget again. Tobey smelled like the perfect mixture of passion and heat and masculinity all rolled up in one.

Callie froze in place, unable to get her limbs to work. She couldn't believe that Tobey's first image of her outside of the wedding refrigerator was like this—could she be any less feminine, she wondered dejectedly—in her own damn commercial refrigerator. Her face, she was sure, was going to be flushed a deep shade of red when she finally stood back up, considering that the man she had been lusting after for the past twenty-four hours had just walked into her store unannounced, just in time to witness her pawing through her shelves on her hands and knees with her ass sticking straight up in the air.

"On second thought," he said, his voice washing over her like hot caramel, "I think I like it."

For a millisecond, Callie considered trying to crawl onto the shelf, hoping that Tobey would just go away. Then again, she thought, she hadn't invited him to her store. In fact, she hadn't even told him she had a store, so how could it possibly be her fault that he had found her looking less than ideal.

Trying desperately to rouse up some anger—otherwise she was stuck with embarrassed and horny, and that was a terrible combination—Callie crawled backwards and stood up, brushing invisible specks of dust off her knees and skirt.

Her arms folded across her chest, she said, "What are you doing here?"

Tobey was leaning against the door, looking more gorgeous than any man had a right to in his pin-striped shirt and well-tailored coat and slacks. He grinned widely and Callie wanted to smack the smile from his lips. And kiss him senseless, of course, but she was going to have some control over herself if it killed her.

"This is Callie's Candies isn't it?"

Callie nodded, keeping her lips firmly pressed together, forcing herself to back up into the refrigerator shelves, rather than jump Tobey's bones like the slut that she was turning out to be.

Tobey smiled. "I'm here for our appointment."

Callie's mouth dropped open. She quickly shut it, but no question about it, her brain wasn't firing correctly anymore. She couldn't manage anything better than, "For our appointment?" She was utterly mortified, sure that her skin was turning pinker and pinker by the second. If things got any worse, she would definitely fade away completely into the fabric of her pink suit.

"10 a.m., Monday morning. My assistant set it up with your accountant."

"You can't be. I mean, you couldn't be. Oh god," she said, leaning her weight into the cool air of the refrigerator as the full ramifications of her actions came crashing down upon her.

Thoughts rushed around her brain, knocking into each other as the magnitude of her mistake sunk in. *I slept with the Candy King. I had a one-night stand with the one person who could save my business. Oh god, what am I going to do? What if he thinks I knew who he was all along and did it on purpose?*

Trying to think quick, she said, "Oh yes, of course. I was so wrapped up in doing my weekly inventory that I forgot all about our appointment." Her voice was as crisp as she could make it, but to her ears her words still sounded far too much like soggy pie crust. Struggling to sound impersonal, she said, "Please forgive me. You're with Sweet…"

Callie let her voice drop and looked up towards the ceiling as if she obviously knew the name of his company but had momentarily forgotten it. She hoped against hope that he would fall for her act.

The truth was, she was such a bad business owner she didn't even know the name of the company that had been sent in to save her from ruin.

"Sweet Returns," he said smoothly, his eyes running past her flushed face to her chest and getting stuck there.

"And of course," he added, never taking his eyes from her breasts, his voice husky and full of the very need she herself was trying to fight off, "I forgive you."

Too late Callie realized that she was flashing Tobey through the translucent white silk of her flimsy camisole. She crossed her arms across her chest, wanting to hide her telltale arousal from Tobey, but it was no use. With her arms crossed beneath her breasts, the soft flesh rose indecently up out of the v-neck top of her skimpy shell. She didn't know which was worse: her hard, pink nipples shooting through the fabric like darts, or the bounteous mounds of her breasts spilling from her top.

Wishing she weren't always doing the wrong thing at the wrong time, Callie bit her lip and said, "Should we get down to business?"

No matter how hard she tried to act professional, her voice was tentative and breathy. Callie knew she sounded like she'd rather get kissed by Tobey than look at the bottom line with him. But she couldn't help it. Tobey was so damn gorgeous. And sexy. And…

Oh my god, he was standing right in front of her. The next thing she knew, he had crossed the small space between them in the storeroom. With the intimacy that comes from knowing just how a woman needs to be touched, he brushed back a curl from her cheek. Callie shivered.

Just like the visions that had kept her awake all night long, Tobey was right there within stroking distance. She needed him desperately. Against any good sense she had ever possessed, her arms uncrossed and moved across his shoulders to entwine around his neck and she pressed her breasts up against his hard chest. "Callie," he said. The word wrapped around her like a deep fog and then his mouth was on hers and her lips were open and greedy and she was moaning. He felt so good, so damn good, she was nearly sobbing with need.

Tobey sucked at her lower lip, letting his teeth graze her skin, still sensitive from their lovemaking at the wedding, before moving his mouth down past her chin and then the side of her neck.

"I was awake all night dreaming about doing this again." He sank his lips into the crook of her neck and sucked at it. Callie groaned.

"Me too," she admitted, unable to stop the confession from rolling off of her tongue.

"And this," he said. He hooked his thumb under the strap of her sheer camisole and slid it off one shoulder, baring the top of her breast to him. Gently he rubbed the soft flesh of her breasts and then bent his head and sucked at the soft tissue. Callie felt her nipples jut out even further, she heard herself crying out his name as she let her neck fall back and pressed her tits into his eager mouth.

She had forgotten everything—where she was, that she hardly knew Tobey, that she was a good girl, the kind of girl who had a good time in bed, but at least the good time had always been in a bed. All Callie cared about was the feel of Tobey's lips and tongue and teeth on her breasts, the way his light stubble felt sandy against her soft skin, the way his hands were cupping her ass, molding her hips into his hardness, just the way she wanted.

Her hands reached for his coat and she roughly pulled it off of his shoulders and threw it on the floor, her mouth taking his, her tongue plunging in and out of his mouth, mating frantically with his. Needing to touch his naked skin more than she needed to breathe, Callie pulled his shirt out from his pants, finally sighing with pleasure when her fingers found the warm, rippling muscles on his back.

With his foot, Tobey closed the door to the storeroom and spun them around, pressing Callie up against it. She felt Tobey's hardness, still covered by his wool slacks, press into her panties, which were already wet with her need. The wool felt rough and scratchy through the thin silk of her panties and she ground her hips into his. Callie felt desperate for release, on the verge of coming apart against Tobey's hard, hot thighs.

"Go on, sweetheart," Tobey urged her.

Callie opened her eyes and she looked into his, dark with passion. Passion for her. It was her undoing.

She threw her head back and Tobey's mouth found the wildly beating pulse in her neck. One hand found her clit, hard and throbbing and ready to explode, the other her aching nipples. One touch, then two and she was gone, exploding against him, shoving her hips into his hands, against his hard cock again and again.

Somewhere in her fog she realized that his hand had dropped from her breast and that his pants had fallen to the floor and he had rolled a condom on. But all she cared about was the hot, stretching sensation at the opening of her vagina, that Tobey was about to plunge his thick penis into her.

All night long Callie had dreamt about Tobey fucking her again, about riding his shaft and crying out his name. She felt him slide into her, sure and fierce, and she found his lips again, wanting to show him how much she loved the way she felt when he was touching her.

She tasted his lips, his tongue, his mouth. "Callie," he groaned, her name sounding like worship, and all of Callie's visions from the sleepless night before merged with their sweaty sex in the refrigerator and the tequila shots and her rubbing herself in the shower dreaming of Tobey.

Her muscles clenched around his cock and she sobbed into his mouth, his tongue pumping in and out of her mouth in the same rhythm that he was thrusting into her. Callie clung to Tobey, her eyes clenched shut, never wanting to wake up from the best dream she had ever had.

"Miss Callie?"

A small voice from the hallway was calling out her name, but Callie was too busy throwing herself at Tobey, too intent on coming against Tobey, to hear.

Tobey called out, "Callie will be out in a minute." Her legs were shaky and she felt so helpless all of a sudden that she stood completely still while Tobey righted all of her clothes. Pushing her hair back from her face and tucking it behind her ears, he said, "That was wonderful, sweetheart."

Callie blushed, feeling suddenly sick at her out-of-control behavior and bent down to pick up Tobey's jacket so that she wouldn't have to look him in the eye. She handed it to him and Tobey quickly rearranged his own clothes then stepped back from the door to give Callie room to open it.

Jonah, a ten–year-old whose mother owned a gift shop on the other end of Main, poked his woolen capped head into the storeroom. He beamed when he saw Callie.

"My mom needs a box of truffles for her store and she sent me over here to see if you could give me some before we open. I sure am glad you're here or else I'd have to ride my bike all the way down here again later."

Callie suddenly saw herself through the innocent eyes of a child and she couldn't help but feel dirty. Forcing herself to ignore Tobey's presence in the room, she walked through the doorway on shaky legs. Laughing, the sound obviously forced, she ruffled Jonah on the head. She kept her voice light and said, "Oh no, Jonah. I'd hate for you to have to ride your bike all the way down Main Street. Again."

Callie heard the trembling behind her teasing words and hated herself for it. She was sure that Tobey could hear it too. Why, she wondered, couldn't she be calm, cool, and collected around him? Why did she have to be so pathetically *attracted* to him?

On the way into the front of her shop, she grabbed her jacket from her office chair and put it back on, wishing she had stayed with her plan of keeping it on, no matter what. If she had known she was meeting with Tobey she would have worn her most chaste outfit, something from the back of closet that covered every square inch of skin from her chin to her ankles.

Callie buttoned the one button at the waist and wondered how she could have ever possibly felt stern and business-like in the suit. Wearing this suit was, she now realized, as good as wearing a sign that said, "Fuck me, please. I like sex with men I don't know." What she wouldn't give for a coat of armor now.

She pulled a large chocolate box off of the shelf and handed it to Jonah. "Why don't you pick out your favorites, honey?" she said, knowing that her hands would be shaking so hard she'd barely be able to get the truffles into the box.

Candy Store

Jonah gave her a look of surprise, but quickly stripped off his mittens and got to work loading up mint and dark chocolate truffles into the box. Even as she chose a lollipop for Jonah from her stash of goodies below the cash register, Callie was far too aware of Tobey's large, hot presence behind her. Everything about him radiated power and sex, all of the stuff she had always been a sucker for.

And look what it had gotten her so far, she reminded herself harshly. She was alone and broke, with nothing but a failing candy store and a mutt to keep her company.

"Miss Callie, I'm done now," Jonah said, snapping her out of her self-pity. "Here," he said, putting a $20 bill in Callie's hand.

She put the bill away in the cash register then handed the little boy his special treat.

"My favorite!" he exclaimed as he shoved the lollipop into the pocket of his down jacket. "Thanks, Miss Callie," he added, getting on his tippy toes to give her a peck on the cheek before he ran out of the heated store into the cold and shot back down Main Street on his bike.

Callie's heart swelled with love. What she wouldn't give to have a child of her own. But since that obviously wasn't about to happen any time soon, she thought, at least she had her candy store and the joy of being with children every day.

"Cute kid," Tobey said, walking around the front of her display counters to check out her displays.

Callie jumped. She had almost forgotten that Tobey was there, invading her sanctuary with his ungodly sexiness. And she had almost forgotten, yet again, that her beloved store was in danger.

And only The Candy King could save her.

Enough is enough, she told herself firmly, her heart fluttering just because of Tobey's intense presence in her store. *You need to focus on business, not pleasure*, she insisted, trying to get the wayward slut inside of her to obey her serious dictate.

"Do you always give away candy like that?" Tobey's tone was light, but she sensed an edge behind his words

"Of course I do," she replied. She hated that she felt like she needed to explain herself, but she said, "Kids love getting a little surprise."

Tobey stopped his perusal of her storefront. "And you like to surprise them?" he asked, pinning her with his hot gaze.

Callie swallowed convulsively, but her mouth felt dry and her tongue refused to fit within the confines of her mouth. All she could do was nod.

The silence in Callie's Candies was almost a live being. Callie wished she knew what happened to her when Tobey was near, that way she might have had a chance in hell at fighting it.

But when he finally said, "I like that about you, Callie. I like that a lot," she knew she was irrevocably lost.

"Lock the door," she said, then turned and walked back into her storeroom. She heard the lock click shut and undid the button on her jacket. Shrugging out of the pink wool, she threw it onto her desk.

She reached for the zipper on her skirt just as Tobey walked through the door. Still unable to look him in the eye, she let her skirt drop to the floor. Standing before Tobey in her see-through white silk camisole and white silk thong panties, she said, "One more time. And then we'll take care of business."

Chapter Four

"Remind me again," Callie said as she stamped her feet in the snow to stay warm. "Why are we doing this?"

Tobey laughed and put the huge cooler he had been carrying into the snow on the edge of the rink. "Ice skaters love two things," he said, taking a moment to admire how cute Callie looked in her form fitted pink down jacket and tight black ski pants. "Perfect ice, obviously, and, even more importantly, chocolate."

Callie humphed and rubbed her mittened hands together. "If I weren't so cold I might care."

Tobey wanted to say, "I've got a surefire way to warm you up," but he knew that given their business relationship, such obvious flirting was totally out of line. Even more than that, though, he wanted to suck that pouty lower lip of Callie's into his mouth.

It really was too bad that after leaving Callie's Candies on Monday, after their crazy, perfect sex on the steel kitchen island in the middle of her store's back kitchen, Tobey felt he had to make the only decision possible under the circumstances—to back off until Callie's Candies was back in the black and running smoothly. It was perfectly all right to fuck Callie's brains out before they discussed business, but once the first professional word had been spoken, Tobey felt that not touching Callie was the right thing to do. Not, of course, that he would hesitate to rip all of her clothes off and keep her naked in his bed for a week once their business transaction had ended.

But for the time being, the last thing Tobey wanted was for Callie to think that the success of her business was in any way linked to whether or not she put out. For the past fifteen years he had always been the consummate professional with his clients. He didn't mix business with pleasure, although, truth be told, he had never been tempted to lick cocoa powder off one of his clients before. In any case, given that this was his very last job in the candy business before the world of accounting took him in, he felt an even greater motivation to do his very best.

Not to mention the fact that he had a very strong personal interest in his gorgeous, talented, oh-so-fuckable client.

So he was going to stick to his decision. Even if it killed him. And just looking at the way Callie's ass rounded up at him as she bent over to unlatch the cooler, Tobey was pretty damn sure that keeping his hands off the delectable little candy maker was, indeed, going to destroy him.

But what a way to go.

After their "meeting" on Monday, Tobey had spent the week holed up in his office day and night, working up a plan of money-making action for her. After looking through her books, he saw that although she was doing fairly well in sales, she was in such a high-rent district that she'd have to either move to another town or double her daily sales.

Their conversation on this matter had been short and sweet.

Tobey: "Have you thought about moving to another location?"

Callie: "No."

Tobey: "The rent is lower and you wouldn't have to worry about losing your shop."

Callie: "I grew up here and I'm staying here. Isn't it your job to figure out a way to make that work?"

Tobey grinned. Just looking at Callie, all blonde and small and round and pink, her fiery, sharp mind wasn't inherently obvious. But it was there. Along with her ravenous sensuality. He couldn't wait to finish the job so that he could get another taste of her incredible lovemaking.

Plans for saving Callie's Candies consumed him. He had already had a web site built for her at a reduced rate by his sister-in-law, who was one of the best in the business, by promising her all the truffles she could eat for the next decade. He was planning on trying the same trade with a hot public relations firm. Next week, he was going to look into national distribution through the major gourmet food chain stores.

In any normal consultation situation, Tobey would have met with her again in person to run his ideas by her, but the sad truth was that he knew he wouldn't be able to control himself around her. Callie had said, "I want to focus on making candy," and so Tobey was able to justify his unorthodox behavior of making do with phone calls by telling himself that it was how she wanted things to be.

Somewhat wryly, he admitted that he might as well have met with Callie in person, considering that even though they had been apart for nearly a week he had been possessed by visions of her. Naked thighs and breasts spread across satin sheets. In the shower with soap suds dripping from her nipples.

Tobey shook the vision from his head and went to work unrolling the new banner that spelled out www.calliescandies.com. He hung it from the roof of the gazebo where he and Callie were setting up shop. The gazebo was situated on the far edge of the large outdoor ice skating rink in Saratoga, less than a mile from the world famous racetracks. Based on his experience of taking his nieces and nephews skating over the years, Tobey knew that on Saturdays and Sundays in January, the rink was packed with kids of all ages and their parents. The perfect audience to spread the word about Callie's incredible confections.

Tobey stepped back to make sure that the banner was straight. Callie stepped beside him and he swore she was searing him even through all of their layers of clothes, even though it was freezing outside.

"I'm still not sure about the web site," Callie said. "Wouldn't people rather come into the store?"

Feeling incredibly protective towards his luscious client, Tobey wanted to allay her fears. "You've got a great store, Callie. It's warm and inviting and who can resist your little surprises?" he said with a small suggestive smile.

Tobey saw the responsive spark in Callie's eyes and caught himself just in time before he lost sight of business altogether. *Focus, buddy. Focus.*

He cleared his throat. "But what about people who don't live in Saratoga and can't get to your store on a regular basis?"

Callie looked confused. "How would they even find out about my store in the first place?"

"You see all of these people out here today?" Tobey asked, gesturing to the growing crowd of skaters that were sliding across the ice. "People are willing to drive quite a distance to skate at such a great outdoor rink. Not to mention the fact that locals often have friends or relatives visiting them for the holidays from out of town."

"And these people will love my truffles and hot cocoa so much that they'll want to order more from my web site when they get home?"

"Exactly," Tobey said, pleased that Callie was letting herself be open to the array of possibilities for her business.

Shyly she looked at him. "Thanks," she said, her lips turning up in an uncertain smile. "I never would have thought to do any of this without you. The web site. Being here today. Getting plans together for a special Valentine's Day gift box. It would have all seemed so hard without you."

Tobey tried to mask his delight at her thank you. He strode over to the cooler and opened it up, pulling out boxes of truffles and putting them on their sales table.

Callie had no idea what hard was. Not in the least. His cock was huge and ready to plunge into her cunt. Even during their brief phone calls, he had gotten so overheated he'd had to walk out of his office in just his shirt and slacks until the cold weather had frozen him completely through. Only then could he concentrate on business again.

Thirty minutes later, just before the doors to the rink opened up to the crowd that had gathered in the parking lot outside, Tobey and Callie had finished setting up the temporary Callie's Candies booth, complete with steaming hot cocoa and truffles in ten different flavors. Callie had packed toffees, taffies and lollipops into small wicker baskets on the table.

They took a few steps back to check over their candy display.

"Looks great," Callie said, not quite meeting his eyes.

Tobey nodded and smiled at the top of her head. "It certainly does. The table is colorful and inviting. I'm certain that Callie's Candies is going to make a huge splash with both the locals and the out-of-towners today."

Callie walked back to the table and fussed needlessly with the display. Tobey knew she was feeling nervous around him.

The problem was, everything was said that needed to be said, and yet none of the important things were being said at all. Thus, an uncomfortable silence fell between them.

It was taking every ounce of control for Tobey to keep his mind on business, when all he really wanted to do was strip off Callie's winter clothes. It was so cold he was starting to add intense visions about hot tubs and saunas to his previous beach and bikini fantasies.

Not for the first time that day, Tobey gave thanks that they were conducting their business together in the frigid outdoors. He didn't think he could keep himself from tearing her clothes off if they were alone and indoors. Even as it was, the cold wasn't working its magic on his overcharged libido.

Callie's pull was just too damn strong.

* * * * *

Callie looked at her watch and prayed that her twelve-year-old niece would show up already. She had asked Ellen to help them sell candy as a buffer. Being alone with Tobey was harder than she had ever thought it would be. And she had thought that it was going to be pretty damn hard.

He was so dark and tall and gorgeous, her breath caught in her chest every time she looked at him. She wanted to drag him behind a tree and pull him down onto the fresh snow with her. She wanted to feel his heavy weight on her, his thick penis plunging in and out of her.

But it didn't matter what Callie wanted. Simply put, the facts were not in her favor.

Fact: He was her hired consultant. It would be morally wrong for her to engage in sexual acts with one of her employees. Under no circumstances did she want him to feel that he had to sleep with her or else she'd bad mouth him in the candy industry.

Fact: He wasn't the least bit interested in her anyway, so all of the high and mighty morals she was desperately trying to cling to didn't matter for much at all. She would have had to have been blind not to notice that since the day they had fucked in her kitchen, he had made it a point to keep away from her. Even his phone calls were oh-so-brief, as if he could hardly stand to talk to her again. Every time she thought about the way she had stuck her tongue down his throat in her store, with absolutely no provocation on his part, every time she remembered the way she had stripped off her clothes and begged him to touch her, Callie felt more and more ashamed by her behavior.

"Aunt Callie, I'm here."

Callie spun around and hugged her little teenage salvation just a little too hard.

"Ouch."

"Sorry, honey. I'm just so glad to see you."

Ellen raised an eyebrow, looking far older than twelve. "Yeah. Whatever. Hey," she said, elbowing Callie in the ribs, "who's the hot guy? Your new boyfriend?"

Callie turned a hundred shades of pink. "No," she insisted, but Tobey was already making the introductions.

"I'm Tobey," he said, as he reached out his hand to shake Ellen's. "I've been working with Callie on her business. I'm a candy company consultant."

Ellen smiled and then looked back at Callie. "That's cool. I'm Ellen," she said. Callie thought she was off the hook, but then Ellen added, "I just thought you were her new boyfriend or something, 'cause she always goes for guys who look like you."

Tobey grinned and trapped Callie with his hot gaze before turning back to Ellen for more information. "So Callie likes guys who look like me, huh?"

Ellen shrugged. "Big. Brown hair. Lots of muscles. They usually treat her like dirt, though, so I guess it's a good thing you aren't her boyfriend after all." Not realizing that she'd said anything out of line at all, Ellen turned to Callie, "So, what do you need me to do?"

Callie was having trouble keeping on her feet at that moment, so she certainly couldn't open up her mouth to reply. Tobey, bless his heart, stepped in and saved her.

"We need your help selling the candy and the hot cocoa on the table. Make sure that you tell everyone who buys something about the web site and hand them one of Callie's cards."

Ellen nodded. "That sounds easy." She looked up and saw the web site address on the banner. "When did you get a web site, Callie? I'll check it out when I get home. You're practically gonna be famous now."

Callie still couldn't get any of her synapses to fire. Ellen's words kept playing in her head. *They usually treat her like dirt, so I guess it's a good thing you aren't her boyfriend after all.*

Was she really that bad at choosing boyfriends? How sad it was that she was only getting a clear picture of her bad choices out of the mouth of a babe.

The doors to the rink opened and within a matter of minutes, Callie, Tobey and Ellen were swarmed with skaters. People started with the hot chocolate to try and warm up, but then after they exclaimed with rapture over the exotic flavor of Callie's cocoa, and after the adults inquired about purchasing the mix to take home, people turned to truffles and toffee and taffy. Tobey made several trips to Callie's car as their boxes of backup supplies quickly disappeared. Between bites of candy and sips of cocoa, Callie heard snippets of conversation: "Did you know that she has a web site?" and "I'm going to tell all of my friends out in California about her." and "This is the best truffle I've ever had. I wonder if she does gift baskets?"

Between sales Callie stole glances at Tobey. Her breath went as she watched him joke with the customers. He was so warm and engaging, he had everyone eating out of his hands. She had to hand it to him. He had most certainly earned his Candy King title. His love for candy came through in everything he did and his quick mind and charming personality sealed the deal.

It was too bad he obviously didn't want to kiss her ever again. Because she couldn't think of anything she wanted to do more.

* * * * *

Several hours later, when the initial crowds had finally died down and Callie was busy mixing up a new batch of hot cocoa, Tobey whispered to Ellen, "Can you hold down the fort for a little while? Your Aunt Callie didn't want to leave you here all alone, but she's been dying to go ice skating with me. And you've been doing the best job out of the three of us. I know a candy selling natural when I see one."

Ellen nodded, clearly pleased to be left in charge of the Callie's Candies booth. "Sure thing, Tobey," she whispered back. "By the way, I think Aunt Callie kind of likes you."

"Really?" he whispered back, enjoying the conspiracy. "What makes you say that?"

"Every time she looks at you she gets all dreamy eyed."

Tobey grinned and started to get up, but Ellen grabbed the elbow of his jacket. "You're not gonna break her heart too, are you?"

Tobey sat back down, suddenly serious. "I don't intend to."

Ellen stared him down and he was surprised by the intensity in her young eyes. "Promise? 'Cause I really like you."

Callie's niece sure loved her, Tobey thought, to be giving out such stern warnings to prospective boyfriends. His face solemn, he said, "I promise. And I really like you too."

Ellen grinned and turned to greet a new customer who had just walked up to the table. Tobey waited until Callie put the top back on her metal pot of cocoa and then grabbed her hand.

"What's going on?" she asked, trying to pull her hand back out of his. "Where are we going?"

Over his shoulder he said, "It's time for a little break, Miss Callie."

"A break? Now? But what about Ellen?"

"Ellen's got it covered. Now tell me," he said, "What size are you?"

Callie flushed and looked down at her chest. "What size am I? What kind of a question is that?"

Tobey mock-leared at her breasts. "Get your mind out of the gutter, Miss Callie." She turned pink and he said, "What size shoe do you wear?"

"Six, but what does it have to do with..." Her words fell away as he let go of her hand and picked up one set of rental skates in a six for her and twelve for himself. Dangling the skates from his fingertips he said, "You and I are going skating."

Callie shook her head. "I don't think so."

Tobey grabbed her hand again and steered her over to a bench. "Put 'em on. Consultant's orders."

Callie giggled uncertainly, but took the skates from him. Staring at them, she said, "I haven't skated in years."

"No time like the present," Tobey said, as he quickly removed his shoes and slipped his feet into the skates. "Besides, you deserve a reward for all of your hard work today."

Tobey hoped that Callie would let herself have a little fun. With him. He saw her shoulders relax a little and breathed out an inaudible sigh of relief. And when she shot him her pixie grin, he made a new decision — to forget all about his earlier decision about not mixing business with pleasure.

If ever there was a time for pleasure, it was now.

And by god, he was going to take it.

* * * * *

Callie had just finished tying the laces on her skates when Tobey whirled her out onto the crowded ice skating rink. Her legs wobbled beneath her and she found herself holding onto Tobey just a little too tightly.

"I need to get my skating legs back," she said by way of explanation, letting herself enjoy the feel of Tobey's warmth pressed up against hers while she could. He had one arm firmly wrapped around her waist and she could feel his warm breath on her forehead. His arms were heaven to her.

"No rush," he said, pulling her closer to him.

They skated several circles around the rink in a comfortable rhythm and for the first time all day Callie let down her guard. If she was able to contain her raging hormones even now, she thought she just might be able to keep it together until she could get home and play with the new dildo she had bought on Tuesday. Cold vibrating plastic wasn't nearly as good as Tobey, but Callie was realistic enough to accept that it would have to do.

Suddenly, Tobey steered them over to the far, deserted edge of the rink and pointed to the sky. "Did you see that bald eagle over there?"

"Where?" Callie shaded her eyes with her hands, but all she could see on the pine trees was white powder from the fresh snowfall.

"In the forest. Come with me."

Tobey grabbed her hand and pulled her into the dense forest with him. Callie's skates sank into the snow, but Tobey was moving so fast, she didn't have a chance to get stuck as she tried to keep up.

By the time he stopped, they were far enough from the skating rink that the sounds of children playing had completely faded away. Not letting go of her hand, he turned and looked into her eyes. "I guess he flew away."

Callie found herself laughing. "Was there really a bald eagle out here?"

Tobey pulled her into him and leaned his face down close to hers. "Maybe there was, but all I've been able to focus on today is you."

Callie breathed in his scent, unable to mask the raw need his words aroused. "Don't tease me Tobey," she said, her voice thick.

"Not even if it makes you feel good?"

"How good?"

Callie felt the familiar liquid rush building up between her legs, pooling at the tip of her breasts.

"Let me show you."

He guided her over to a patch of ground far beneath the huge canopy of an oak tree and pressed her back into the bark of the tree, then leaned into her, shielding her from the cold. "One day we're going to have to do this lying down. Properly. Warm and cozy in bed."

Callie shivered at the thought of getting to do this with Tobey one more time. In a bed, even. It was too delicious to believe. But then again so was the velvet feel of his lips as they stole her breath away. Feeling bold, she said between kisses, "I like doing it standing up. I like being bad with you."

Tobey smiled against her lips. "Me too, sweetheart. I love the way you wrap your legs around me. How slick you get when I'm pumping in and out of you. How ready you are for me all the time."

Callie swallowed and licked her lips. "I'm ready now," she whispered.

Deftly he threw his gloves to the ground and unbuttoned the fly on her snow pants. Unzipping them, he slid his warm hands onto the soft skin of her belly. "I need to see if you're telling the truth," he said as his hand dropped another inch, just grazing the edge of her already damp mons. "Mmm," he murmured against her ear lobe, sucking it into his mouth, "good so far."

The feel of his mouth against her brought goose bumps to her skin that had nothing to do with the cold. She arched her hips into his hands, forcing his fingers to slide across her swollen nub into her wet folds. "Oh god," she moaned.

"I want to see you come again, Callie," he said. He made several slow, torturous circles on her clit and then slipped his fingers down into her labia, finally pushing her open with one thick finger.

Callie drove her hips into his hand.

"Come for me, sweetheart," he said against her lips and Callie, who wanted to please him more than anything else in the world, felt everything inside and outside of her go perfectly still, as if the whole universe was waiting for her to explode.

Tobey's hand stilled. He looked into her eyes. One simple word, "Now," was all it took. She closed her eyes as the earth starting spinning fast, too fast. She came out of her body and lifted higher and higher. Everything turned red, then black, as pleasure coursed through her. And then she was kissing Tobey and he was kissing her back, their lips mating in perfect rhythm to her waves of ecstasy.

Tobey quickly stripped off his winter coat and laid it on the ground, seemingly impervious to the cold. Gently, he lowered Callie onto it. She lay back on her elbows and looked at him, excitement making her breath come out in short, quick white puffs of air.

"I wish I could take off all of your clothes and see you naked," he said as he pulled her pants and soaked panties down far enough to spread her thighs.

"Later," she moaned, not feeling the least bit inhibited about lying in the snow in the forest, naked from her waist to her ankles.

Tobey nodded. "Later," he echoed as he bent his head over her mound, lapping at her sweetness with his tongue. He ran his tongue up her lips, from her anus to her clit, giving equal importance to every square inch of engorged flesh.

Callie arched up into his mouth. She felt like she could come and come and come and come and it still wouldn't take the edge off her arousal.

Tobey slipped his tongue inside of her vagina in one firm, long stroke and then another. Callie gasped and her muscles clenched around his tongue. His thumb found her clit and he plunged his tongue in and out of her as he swirled her firm bead.

She cried out as the orgasm ripped through her, her cries muted by the thick canopy of the pine tree. Tobey replaced his tongue with two fingers and sucked her clit into his mouth, faster and faster, harder and harder. Callie writhed beneath him, her fingers tangled in his thick brown hair as she pushed his mouth harder to her. She was tumbling through space, dizzy with pleasure.

Tobey reared up over Callie, pushing her thighs open just a little more so that he could kneel between her legs. Callie opened her eyes and saw his perfect cock, so hard and pushing out from his dark pubic hair, already sheathed within a condom. She wanted to reach out her hand to stroke him, to fill her small hand with the heavy weight of his shaft, but before she could even think about taking off her gloves, he was unzipping her coat and running his hands over her turtleneck, teasing her taut peaks and plunging his hips into hers.

"Squeeze your thighs together," he said.

Callie barely managed to obey him, she was so concentrated on the feel of Tobey over her. On her. In her. She wrapped her hands around his shoulders to pull him closer to her while she squeezed her thighs together as tight as she could.

She felt his cock growing impossibly bigger within her with every stroke and suddenly she was floating and he was coming and saying her name and she was moving with him, bucking her hips up off the blanket of his jacket, trying to get closer to him, as close as she could possibly get.

* * * * *

Afraid of crushing Callie, Tobey tried to prop his weight up on his forearms, but she was holding him so tightly to her that he decided to just let himself go.

He rolled them over slightly, so that he was cradling her in his arms, their bodies still joined together. The truth hit him like a bolt of lightning.

He was in love with her.

He had never been so sexually compatible with any woman, but it was more than just the sex that made him so positive that Callie was the one. She was funny and bright and just seeing her smile made him want to do or say something to make her smile again.

Callie's breathing began to slow to normal and he rubbed her back, savoring the feeling of having found the woman he wanted to spend the rest of his life with.

He knew they needed to get back to the rink, but he didn't want to move too fast, to fall back into real life. He slowly pulled out and zipped his pants back up.

Callie blinked and then fumbled for her snow pants. Pulling her to her feet, Tobey took care of getting her back in order within seconds.

He took her face in his hands and kissed her, long and slow and sweet with all of the love he had in him. "This isn't a one-night stand," he said, his voice firm and tender all at the same time.

Callie smiled back at him and covered his hands with her own. "I know."

Chapter Five

The next two weeks were the best weeks of Callie's life. After their incredible lovemaking in the forest, they had gone back to the rink to pack up her sales table. Much to Callie's surprise, Tobey had insisted that they talk about their relationship. She had never met a man like him before, one who was willing to broach difficult subjects. Every man she'd ever known before had hidden from emotions, had ignored anything that wasn't cut and dry.

"I want to date you," he said, and she said, "Me too."

"I know I'm working for you," he said, and she said, "And I've hired you."

"I want to be your lover as well as your business associate," he said, and she said, "Thank god."

They had both laughed and suddenly the air was clear and full of endless possibilities.

Not only was Callie constantly glowing with joy, but her business was growing by leaps and bounds as well, with a huge spike in business from Internet orders.

One night after a romantic dinner at her house where they had done more hand-holding and kissing than eating, Callie said, "You really are the Candy King, you know," her tone teasing.

Tobey stiffened slightly at her words, but then relaxed again so quickly she was certain that she had imagined it.

"How did you know that you were so darn good at selling candy?" she asked.

Tobey kissed her on her neck, right below her ear, in just the way that was guaranteed to make her nipples hard and aching. "You don't want to hear about my boring business," he said, trying to coax her into another incredible sexual interlude, his palm coming to cup her between her thighs, searing her with his heat even through her jeans.

But even though Callie was already responding to his touch, her breasts heavy, her mons throbbing, Callie had had enough of his putting her off. Last night after making love in her bathtub, she had finally realized that whenever she asked him questions about his company, he deftly changed the subject. Usually by kissing or touching her, until she was naked and coming beneath him, all thoughts of business gone.

Callie scooted away from Tobey on the couch, hating how empty she felt without his touch, but knowing they needed to have this conversation more than they needed to have sex. "Why do you keep pushing me away?"

Tobey looked at the empty place on the couch where Callie had been just seconds before and then up at Callie, now several feet away from him. His voice gruff, he said, "What are you talking about?"

Callie sighed. "Every time I bring up your business, you change the subject. For the past two weeks all we've talked about is Callie's Candies." Her voice softened. "I want to find out more about you, Tobey."

When she felt Tobey tense, Callie scooted back into the circle of his arms and planted several kisses on his forearms and hands, pulling his strong arms around her. Tobey's muscles relaxed slightly. But still, he didn't offer Callie any information about his past.

Trying to hide her growing exasperation, Callie said, "What was your favorite kind of candy when you were a kid?"

Tobey, who was clearly surprised by her innocuous question, laughed. "That's easy," he said, as he let his guard down. "Necco Wafers."

Sticking her tongue out, Callie scrunched her face up. "Yuck," she said.

He tickled her stomach playfully and the fuzzy feeling throughout Callie's body intensified. It was taking everything she had not to forget the whole conversation and just fuck his brains out instead. She could feel his large erection pushing into her bottom, and she wriggled up against him.

"They're sweet and sort of chalky," he whispered in her ear. "Just like somebody I know, minus the chalk of course. All sweetness."

Callie sucked in a breath as his fingers moved to the curve of her breast. She laughed, but the sound was breathy and aroused. "That was a close one, buddy," she said. "I don't know any women who like to be compared to tasteless chalk."

Keep him talking, she told herself, but at this point, she wished that he would talk a little faster so that she could tear off all of his clothes and take his cock into her mouth.

Callie had always thought that patience was one of her strong suits—after all, she dealt with children as customers on a daily basis—but in the silence that ensued, where all she could hear was the crackling wood on the fire and Wolf's heavy dog breathing, she realized how wrong she was. She was about to give up on ever finding anything out about Tobey's past when his hand stilled on her breast.

"I worked for Mr. Jonas after school at his grocery store. He had a small candy section in the corner and he put me in charge of it."

Aha, now they were getting somewhere. "Free candy?"

Tobey grinned against the top of her head and he scooted her in more snugly against his lap. "All I could eat. I started arranging things differently, putting up new signs, created some package deals, and by the time I graduated from high school, Mr. Jonas's candy store was about ten times bigger."

"And then?"

He sighed. "And then I went to college, got an MBA with a focus in food retailing, and the rest," he said with a note of finality, "is history. Now let's good to the good stuff."

Callie tilted her head up and reached around behind her to lace her fingers into his thick dark hair. Pressing her lips to his, she kissed him with all of the growing love in her heart. She wasn't ready to say the words to him yet, but every time she touched him she knew that her feelings were obvious.

"Thank you for telling me all that," she said, her lips bruised with their passionate kisses.

Tobey leaned down and licked her full lower lip. "You're welcome, sweetheart."

Callie shivered. She loved it when he called her sweetheart. Even though they'd only been formally dating for two weeks, she felt closer to him than she ever had to another person. She had shared her body and soul with

Tobey and somewhere in the back of her head she knew she wanted to continue doing so for the rest of her life.

She was so relaxed and content in his arms that when he said, "Now is probably a good time to tell you that I'm closing my business and going to work with my brother," she jumped with surprise and the top of her head knocked into his chin, clacking his teeth together.

She spun out of his arms. "You're doing what?"

Tobey's face instantly turned from loving to grim in the space of a heartbeat. "You're my last client."

Callie forgot all about being supportive and gentle in her shock. "Why would you do something like that?"

His eyes steel, he said, "It's time to finally grow up."

"What are you talking about? You have a wonderful business. And from working with you, I know for a fact that you love what you do." She narrowed her eyes. "What are you planning to do instead?"

Tobey nearly winced. "Accounting."

Callie's eyes grew wide. "Excuse me? I must have heard you wrong. I thought my talented, creative boyfriend just said he's going to give up his dream job to go into accounting."

Tobey got up off the couch and headed for the door. "You heard right. My brother Jed is going to bring me into his department." His voice was hard and Wolf, who was lying on the rug in front of the roaring fireplace, whined. Looking angry and hurt, Tobey said, "I'll call you later." He walked out the front door and closed it behind him with a deliberate click.

The tears that were welling in Callie's eyes started to fall. Wolf got up and padded over to her, licking her face several times before plopping his head on her lap.

"I've really blown it this time, Wolf," she said, her heart heavy. "No wonder I always date jerks. The one time I find a great guy I drive him away."

Callie scooted out from underneath Wolf's head. She walked into her kitchen and pulled out the ingredients for cocoa fudge. She knew she wouldn't be able to sleep tonight, not for one single minute, not with the distressed look on Tobey's face playing in her head on repeat every five seconds. The only thing that would keep her from going crazy would be baking. She wiped at the tears on her cheeks and put on her apron.

"Here I am again," she said aloud in her empty kitchen. "Just me, my dog, and sugar."

* * * * *

By the time Tobey got back to his large loft, his anger was gone. All he felt was a deep sense of shame at the way he had treated Callie. She had called him her boyfriend, a word that made him feel better than any industry award ever had, and he had stomped out of her home in a huff.

Idiot.

He dropped his keys onto the slate kitchen island and looked around his home with new eyes. He had always thought that he was suited to the hard lines of glass and concrete and slate, but after spending so much time at both Callie's homey store and her cute cottage on the outskirts of town he found that he was craving softness. And color. And comfort. What he wouldn't give to be back in Callie's house, kissing her in front of the fire, with her big mutt lying at their feet snoring.

Chapter Six

The next day Tobey walked into Callie's Candies holding a bright bouquet of yellow and white narcissus. She was down on the ground with her back to the front door, helping a couple of little girls pick out a gift for their mother's birthday while their father watched with pride.

"Mommies love these boxes of truffles," she said to the girls as she showed them a heart shaped box with a thick velvet ribbon on top.

The two girls solemnly nodded their agreement and handed her a five dollar bill. Just as solemnly, treating them as if they were forty-year-old women buying thousands of dollars of merchandise instead of little kids, Callie took their money and walked around to her register. Tobey noted that her eyes and face looked swollen and puffy and inwardly cursed himself. He had done that to her with his callous, selfish behavior. Right then and there he vowed never to treat her badly ever again.

When Callie looked up and saw him standing awkwardly by the door, holding the flowers as an obvious peace offering, she nearly dropped the box of truffles on the floor. She caught the box in mid-air and placed it on her gift-wrapping table, her hands shaky. She gave him a tremulous smile and was about to say something when Tobey smiled back and leaned against the wall, making it clear that he could wait until she was done helping the girls.

Callie finished wrapping the truffles with trembling fingers. She handed the girls a lollipop each and then followed them with her eyes as they took their father's hand and skipped out the door.

Tobey approached her at the same time that she ran around the counter. Their words intermingled, "I'm so sorry," he said, and she said, "No, I'm the one who's sorry."

He handed her the bouquet and she clutched them to her chest as if they were more valuable to her than gold or diamonds. "Can you forgive me?"

Tobey stroked her cheek with his fingers. "What did I ever do right to deserve you?"

Callie shook her head. "I'm the lucky one. And I want you to know that I'll always support you. Whatever you do, I'll still love you," she said.

She gasped and took a step back into the counter, dropping the flowers onto the floor as she realized what she'd just said.

Tobey closed the space between them, stepping into the circle of flowers on the floor. "I love you too," he said and then dipped his mouth to hers. He buried his hands in Callie's soft curls and tasted her sweetness. Her hands wrapped around him and she pulled him tightly to her. Even the bell ringing on the door to the shop, indicating that a customer had entered, was not enough for either of them to want to pull away from each other.

"Ahem," a firm voice said from behind Tobey's back. He pulled away from Callie's sweet lips and groaned, knowing that voice could only belong to one person.

Looking over his shoulder he said, "Alice."

Shaking her head as if they were two kids goofing around during class, Alice said, "I thought I might find you here."

Callie slid out from Tobey's arms and held out her hand, looking charmingly disheveled. "I've been so looking forward to meeting you, Alice." Callie blushed and said, "Under different circumstances, of course."

Alice yielded slightly under the weight of Callie's charm and shook her hand. Turning back to Tobey, the older woman said, "I'd like to know if you think your behavior is going to sell more candy in this store, or less? You've got an important phone call to return in the office."

Tobey grinned shamelessly and held his hands up in defeat. "Point taken, sergeant." He leaned over the counter and placed another quick kiss on Callie's lips. "Are we still on for dinner tonight? My family has been dying to meet you."

Callie whispered, "I can't wait," and they made do with one more quick peck.

Callie stood in the store alone with Alice, feeling more nervous than she had since she was a schoolgirl. But Alice wasn't one to beat around the bush.

"I'll get straight to the point," Alice said and Callie nodded, her heart pounding even though she knew she hadn't done anything wrong. Trying to break the ice, Callie interrupted and said, "Can I offer you anything first? Maybe some hot cocoa and a truffle?"

Alice looked momentarily flustered. "Why yes," she said. "I could use a hot drink to warm my bones." Callie went to pour her a steaming cup and Alice said, "And if you wouldn't mind, I'd love a truffle. I had one last year and I still haven't forgotten it."

Callie breathed a sigh of relief. Tobey's assistant seemed a whole lot less scary when she had chocolate smudged on her lips. "I didn't mean to interrupt you," she said, after Alice had bitten into the truffle with a sound of delight.

Alice held up her hand, making it clear that she wanted to finish the chocolate in silence. Callie grinned, pleased that her candy made people so happy. But her grin fell away as Alice said, "I wasn't sure that I approved of your relationship with Tobey at first—it is unprofessional for a consultant to date his client, after all—but now I can see that you're the best thing that's happened to him in some time."

Callie was frozen where she stood. Alice continued, "I love him like a son and he's about to make the biggest mistake of his life. I want you to stop him."

Her brain struggled to catch up. "Do you mean how he's closing his business?"

Alice nodded, her lips tight again in disapproval.

"Has he talked to you about it?" Callie asked.

"No. But that boy can't hide anything from me. Never could, never will. I've known for months. But I also know that he hasn't made it official yet by firing me because he doesn't want to shut down his dreams."

Callie shook her head. "Alice, I appreciate you coming here to try and help Tobey, but I don't think he's going to listen to me."

Alice's eyes were bright. "Honey, that's where you're wrong. You could tell him to jump off of a cliff and he'd do it. It's up to you to make sure he doesn't make the biggest mistake of his life. I'm counting on you."

* * * * *

That night as Callie sat in the chic new restaurant surrounded by Tobey's parents and his brother and wife, she was still trying to get Alice's words out of her head. *He doesn't want to do it. It's up to you to make sure he doesn't make the biggest mistake of his life. I'm counting on you.*

Callie tried to focus on getting to know Tobey's relatives, all the while wondering when things had become so complicated. One day she was happily running her business and the next she was dating a passionate, complex man who was turning both her little store and her life upside down. Everything was getting so big, so fast.

Tobey's mother, Joan, turned to her and said, "So you're the famous Callie from Callie's Candies?"

Callie blushed. "I don't know about famous."

Joan waved her hand in the air. "Nonsense. My women's group has been enjoying your truffles for years. And besides," she said, lowering her voice, "John and I haven't heard about anything else for weeks."

Callie stuttered unintelligible monosyllables, but Joan wasn't expecting a response. "John and I think it is just perfect that you and Tobey found each other. Two candy lovers who are obviously in love with each other."

Callie had to clamp her teeth together to keep her mouth from falling open. She tried to smile, but she was sure her attempt looked pathetic. Thankfully, Joan was drawn into a conversation with her husband and Tobey. Callie turned to Tobey's older brother, Jed, with relief.

Jed leered at her and she barely repressed a shudder as she took in his beady eyes, oily hair, and bad breath. His wife, a thin dour woman, sat like a mouse beside him. Her eyes were glassy and Callie didn't envy the woman one bit. "So you own a candy store," he said, more a statement than a question. His words struck her as being almost snide and she was sure that she must have misread his intentions.

"That's right. Callie's Candies is just down the street."

Jed rolled his eyes. "Candy," he scoffed. "Good thing my brother has finally come to his senses."

Callie sucked in a breath. "Excuse me?" she said, her voice soft and still, working hard not to betray her growing anger. How could it be, she wondered, that Tobey and Jed were related by blood? They were polar opposites.

"I've worked on him for years to join me in the accounting firm. Something he'll finally get some respect for. Do you know how embarrassing it is to be related to the Candy King?" The words 'Candy King' sounded like spoilt milk coming out of Jed's mouth.

Callie curled her fingers tightly into her fist, fighting the overpowering urge to punch Tobey's jerk of a brother in his fat mouth.

"No. I don't," she said, deciding her only hope was to humor Jed until dinner was over.

As she nodded in all the right places during Jed's endless discourse on his importance and value as a high-powered accountant, everything became crystal clear to Callie. Jed was jealous of Tobey's success and happiness. Obviously, Jed was the one that had been putting pressure on Tobey to "finally grow up," since Tobey's parents clearly loved and supported him in his career choice. She knew they were proud of him, just as they somehow managed to be proud of their other brute of a son.

It was as if a huge weight was lifted from her shoulders. She knew what she needed to say to Tobey. Maybe, just maybe, she would have a fighting chance at succeeding at convincing him to keep Sweet Returns in business.

Callie planted a smile on her face and knew that nothing else Jed said to her tonight was going to bring her down. She would keep up the small talk when she had to and focus most of her attention on getting to know Tobey's wonderful parents better.

Whatever she had to put up with to be with Tobey was worth it.

* * * * *

Tobey sat back and watched Callie charm his family just as she charmed every single person she came in contact with. Even his brother, who could be somewhat standoffish with strangers, was talking animatedly to her.

"Being the VP at an accounting firm is a big responsibility," Jed said, his chest puffed up with pride at his accomplishments.

Tobey shook his head as he caught snippets of Jed's conversation with Callie. Tobey didn't begrudge Jed any of his success, but sometimes Tobey thought he rode the fine line between pride and arrogance. Thank god, Tobey thought, that Callie didn't care about stuff like that. She just wanted him to be happy.

Callie leaned in towards his brother and said, "Wow. Your job sounds *really* exciting. And important."

Tobey blinked hard a couple of times. What the hell was she saying? Jed's job sounded important? And exciting? Jed said something in response which Tobey couldn't hear, but he couldn't miss Callie's impressed response. "That figure was your bonus for last year? Wow. I didn't know accountants did quite so well."

Suddenly the room felt too small and Tobey grabbed at his tie to loosen it from around his neck. As the awful truth crashed in around him, he could no longer breathe.

He shot up out of his chair without a word to anyone and made it as far as the parking lot before he bowled over into a hedge of snow covered boxwood and threw up. He could hardly believe what he had heard, even though now that he had seen the evidence for himself, there was no denying it.

Callie wasn't the woman he thought she was.

Instead of the cute, sweet, supportive woman he thought he loved, instead of the woman who looked at a bouquet of flowers as more precious than jewels, she was a power-grubbing bitch, just like his ex-fiancée had been.

Tobey got in his Ferrari and sped off into the night, leaving behind the woman who had broken his heart forever.

* * * * *

Callie nodded absently at Jed's bragging—he didn't require any help from her to prod his boasting into the stratosphere—wondering where Tobey had rushed off to without a word to anyone. When he had been gone more than five minutes, she excused herself and asked the host to check the men's restroom. But Tobey was gone.

Callie slumped into the coat rack, wondering what had happened. One minute everything was great, the next minute Tobey was gone. She went back to the table and asked his parents, "Did Tobey say anything to you about needing to leave early?"

His mother and father shook their heads, looking worried. "No. I wonder if something he ate didn't agree with him?"

Callie murmured something that was supposed to be comforting, but her heart wasn't it in. Her boyfriend had walked out on her for the second time in twenty-four hours. She fought back the tears that threatened to spill, not wanting his family to see her looking so pathetic.

Jed, clueless as ever, sneered and said, "Geez. The dumb little brother of mine doesn't even know how to take care of his lady."

Something inside Callie snapped. "You don't know the first thing about your brother," she said and then turned and walked out the restaurant. Once she made it out the front door, she ran down the street until she could find an alley to hide in.

Sniffling, Callie didn't want to give into the awful misery that was sucking her in. He didn't want her. No man who was worth anything had ever wanted her.

Callie had been dumped before, but this time, she realized, everything was different. He had said he loved her. No one had ever said that before.

And by god, she was going to fight for him. Even if it killed them both.

Chapter Seven

Callie walked the three blocks to Tobey's loft in a driving rain. She didn't care that she was getting soaked to the bone. She didn't care that her teeth were shattering. Love like this only came once in a lifetime, and no matter what Callie had to do, she wasn't going to let it go.

Her hand a tight, frozen fist, Callie banged on Tobey's steel door with all of her might. When he didn't answer immediately, she banged again, using the pain of the crashing of her bone and flesh against metal as a reminder of all that she was fighting for. Of what she was fighting against.

The rain poured down on Tobey's front stoop in sheets and still Tobey didn't answer the door. Intent on waiting for him for as long as it took, Callie slid down to the floor, shivering in her thin sheath dress and heels. She wrapped her arms tightly around her and rocked back and forth, finally letting the tears that she had been holding back merge with the streaks of rain across her face.

* * * * *

Tobey pushed his Ferrari as hard as it would go on the farm roads outside of Saratoga. On a night like this, where the hail was as big as his fist, everyone else had the sense to keep off the roads. Which suited Tobey just fine as he watched his speedometer inch past eighty, then ninety, then one hundred. He drove like a madman, heedless of his own safety, until finally he skidded to a stop, narrowly missing both a large deer and a deep ditch.

His heart was pounding in his chest. "No," he cried in the car, the sound harsh and wild, like an animal that has lost its mate. Laughing bitterly at what a fool he had been, not once but twice, he gripped the wheel tightly and skidded back onto the road, heading for home. He was going to drown his sorrow in anything other than tequila—Tobey was never going to drink tequila again, all it did was remind him of Callie's taste, of Callie's treachery—and then he was going to take care of something he had been putting off for too long.

He was going to shut down Sweet Returns.

What did he need with true love and a job he loved anyway, he asked himself.

All they'd ever done was cause him trouble.

Tobey came to a screeching halt in front of his loft and flew out of his car, unable to believe what he was seeing. Callie was curled up like a sick child on his front steps, her eyes clenched tightly shut to keep out the rain, her bare skin full of red welts from the hail.

His anger forgotten in his fear, Tobey ran to her and picked her up in his arms. Murmuring sounds of comfort into her hair, trying desperately to warm her with his heat, he fumbled with the lock in the door. Finally managing to get it open he hurried inside and kicked the door shut.

"I'm so cold, Tobey. So cold," Callie said through the loud clacking of her teeth. Goosebumps covered her skin and Tobey hugged her tighter to him.

"I'm going to run a hot bath for you, sweetheart," he said, flinching as the endearment slipped from his lips.

Nonetheless he felt compelled to comfort her. "Once I take these wet clothes off of you, I promise you'll feel better."

Callie didn't say anything, she just shivered and looked up into his eyes as if she was trying to tell him something important. But Tobey couldn't let himself think about anything other than getting Callie warm. Otherwise he would have to face anger and pain and hurt so strong he thought he might never laugh or smile again.

Sitting on the wide rim of his large whirlpool tub, still cradling Callie in his lap, he leaned over and turned the knobs until steaming water was pouring into the tub. Quickly he stripped her dress off and as he undid the clasp of her bra and slid it from her shoulders, he tried not to notice that her breasts were tight and her nipples were hard buds from the cold. He stripped her panties from her legs and forced himself to ignore the pull her mons had on him, to ignore how much he wanted to bury his face between her lips and taste her one more time to memorize her before he let her go forever.

Gently, Tobey lowered Callie into the tub. His hand brushed the soft mound of her breasts and he heard her gasp. Knowing it was wrong, hating himself for being so out of control, Tobey leaned into her and took one of her nipples in his mouth, suckling hard, wanting to punish and pleasure her in equal parts. Callie arched up into his mouth, and threaded her fingers behind his head.

With a groan that hid none of his anger at himself or at her, he pulled away from her and ripped off his own wet clothes. Callie reached her arms up to him and within seconds he was naked and between her legs and pumping into her.

"I love you, Tobey," she cried as her wet, slick canal throbbed around his cock. Tobey tried to block out her words. He tried to concentrate on the wet warmth that encased his penis, her huge, perfect breasts rubbing against his chest, her round ass in his hands as he pounded in and out of her. But even as he tried to use her for his pleasure, he couldn't escape the truth.

Cupping her cheeks with his hands, Tobey stilled. "I love you," he whispered. "I love you," he said again and then thrust into her hard. In the space of one heartbeat, they both came apart. After the madness had subsided, the water sloshed around them in the tub and Tobey pulled away from Callie.

"Don't leave me again," she said. "We need to talk."

Tobey stood up and water poured off of him into the tub. "Fine," he said, trying to rouse his anger at Callie again. "Talk." He grabbed a towel and roughly dried himself off.

Callie stood up too and grabbed a towel. "Why did you leave the restaurant like that?"

Tobey answered her question with a question. "Why did you lie to me?"

Callie sat heavily on the rim off the tub. "I've never lied to you."

"Bullshit," Tobey said, his eyes flashing dangerously. "I saw the way you were fawning all over my brother." His voice grew high pitched as he imitated her. "Your job sounds really exciting and important." Tobey snarled then resumed his parody. "Wow, I didn't know accountants made so much money."

Callie gasped in outrage. "How dare you make me sound like, like…like such a money-grubbing bitch."

Tobey grabbed her by the shoulders, forcing her to stand face to face with him. "Isn't that what you are?

Haven't you just been playing at being the nice little candy maker, pretending you wanted me to live my dreams, when all along you just wanted money. And power. Just like Gina."

Callie's fighting stance fell away. "Gina? Who's Gina?"

Tobey let go of her shoulders, trying not to wince at the red marks his fingers had left on her smooth skin. "My ex."

Callie's voice was soft. "You've never mentioned any ex before."

His voice low, Tobey said, "She left me at the altar. On the day of our wedding."

Callie took a step closer to Tobey and put her hand on his arm asking, "Why?"

Tobey pushed her comfort away and stepped out of the tub with a harsh laugh. "You should understand her motives perfectly. After all, who would want to be married to the Candy King?"

Callie licked her lips and swallowed once before saying, softly, "I would, Tobey."

Tobey turned back to her, anguish etched in the lines of his face. "No, Callie, you don't. You want me to be just like Jed, just like she did. Just like everyone does."

Carefully stepping out of the tub, Callie came toe to toe with Tobey. "Your brother is jealous of you, Tobey. I was stroking his ego in the hopes that he would shut up so that I could get to know your parents better. I thought you knew me better than that," she said, her voice shaky. "I thought you knew how much I love you for being you."

The tears were rolling down her cheeks and she wiped at them angrily. Everything in her was telling her to run away, to leave Tobey, to give up on them. But Callie knew it was the coward's way out. She had vowed to fight for their love and now she was being put to the ultimate test.

Tobey didn't say anything, he just clenched his eyes shut, so Callie forced herself to keep talking, hoping that she could keep him from leaving again, hoping that something she said would break down the walls of hurt he had built up so long ago.

"I'm not the only one who's proud of you, Tobey. Your parents are incredibly proud of you. Alice loves you like a son and it's been killing her to watch you try and shut down something so beautiful that you created from love."

Tobey's eyes opened with surprise. "How do you know these things?"

Callie reached out a hand to his chin and was so glad when he didn't push her away. "They all love you, Tobey. Just like I do. Even a blind man could see it."

Suddenly, Tobey wrapped his arms around Callie, dragging her breasts against his chest. "What about a stupid man?" he said, his voice husky yet hopeful.

Tears fell down her cheeks. "Even a stupid man," she said as their mouths found each other. "Especially if he's the most amazing, intelligent, loving man I've ever met. Now take me to that bed you always talk so much about and love me."

Chapter Eight

February 14th. Valentine's Day.

Callie opened up her shop and tried not to feel sorry for herself. After all, now that everything was out in the open between her and Tobey, she had everything she'd ever dreamed of and more.

She had true love.

She had a man she could talk to about anything, a partner that she could depend on and who could depend on her.

The only thing she didn't have was a date for Valentine's Day.

Again.

Now that Tobey was committed to keeping Sweet Returns up and thriving as a candy consulting business, he had been setting meetings with all of the potential clients that he had put off for the past several months. It just so happened that he had to fly out for an overnight trip to Chicago on Valentine's Day.

He had been incredibly apologetic and of course Callie had been understanding even though she wanted to beg him to rearrange his schedule. It was all for the best, she told herself. Valentine's was one of her busiest days of the year and each year, by the time she flipped her sign from open to closed, she could barely do more than drag herself off to bed.

Settling into another "Holiday of Love" at her store, Callie did brisk sales all day. With a smile on her face, she sold out of the expensive gift baskets that Tobey had helped her put together and in any spare time she had she filled last-minute orders for chocolate and candy that came in over the Internet.

By 5 p.m. it was completely dark outside and Callie was exhausted. The big rush was through—most people were at home sharing a romantic evening in front of the fire together by now. Callie had been hoping that Tobey would call and wish her a happy Valentine's Day from Chicago, but every time she picked up her phone it was another customer making an order for a box of truffles or a gift basket.

She was on the phone with a long-distance customer when a delivery truck parked outside her store and a man walked in with a vase of roses. And then another. And then another.

Callie quickly wrapped up her call. "Excuse me," she said to the delivery man. "I think you're delivering these roses to the wrong place."

The man looked at his clipboard. "This is Callie's Candies, isn't it?"

Callie nodded, her heart beginning to blossom with joy.

By the time the man drove away, Callie's Candies was filled with vases of roses of every color—on the floor, on the counter, on every shelf. Callie headed for the phone to call Tobey's cell phone to thank him for being the most wonderful boyfriend in the world, but before she could wind through the vases of flowers, four men in tuxedos walked through the door carrying musical instruments.

Hardly able to believe what was happening, the string quartet began to serenade her with her favorite symphony. Tears pooled in her eyes and she had to lean against her display counter to stay steady.

No doubt about it, Tobey was the most romantic, wonderful boyfriend in the whole world. Callie couldn't believe she had doubted him for even one single second. Even from all the way in Chicago, he was giving her the best Valentine's Day she had ever had.

And then her heart stopped as the man she loved walked through the door. She ran into Tobey's arms and he swept her up against him and kissed her passionately.

"Happy Valentine's Day, sweetheart," he said and she kissed him back with all of the love in her heart.

Silently, the string quartet left them alone in Callie's Candies while they gave each other soft kisses and murmured words of love.

"I think we're alone now," Tobey said in a voice laced with passion and love.

"Lock the door," Callie said, wanting to drag Tobey into the back room to rip all of his clothes off and show him just how much his romantic deeds meant to her.

Tobey grinned. "I'm always locking the door when I'm with you."

Callie planted another kiss on his succulent lips and whispered, "That's because I'm always taking off my clothes whenever you're around."

"I knew there was a good reason," Tobey said as he quickly locked the door and pulled down the blinds.

Callie reached for his big warm hands and pulled him into the back room with her. Propping him up against the door, she dropped to her knees and began to undo his belt loop. Tobey laced his fingers through her hair and closed his eyes. In seconds, Callie had his hard, throbbing shaft in her greedy fingers.

"Just what I was looking for," she said, as her hot breath wafted over Tobey's pulsating head. "My big, tasty Valentine's Day treat."

Tobey groaned as Callie tasted him with the tip of her tongue. She took his length into her mouth, sucked and pulsating in a perfect rhythm until he couldn't take it anymore.

Pushing her head away from his cock, he dropped to the floor and had both of their clothes off in record time. Naked, facing each other on their knees, Callie climbed on top of Tobey, setting his penis just at the base of her pussy.

"Will you marry me?" he said, and as she slid down on his cock, taking all of it, loving every inch of it as it throbbed inside her, she said, "Yes," and then everything exploded in the ultimate expression of love. The kind of sweet, passionate love that lasts forever.

Callie's Cocoa Fudge

2/3 cup powdered cocoa

3 cups sugar

1/8 tsp. salt

1-1/2 cups whole milk

4-1/2 T. butter (real butter, not margarine or 'spread')

1 tsp. vanilla

Note: This recipe needs two people to take turns stirring and watching and beating the fudge. Clothing optional—it's going to get *really* hot in here, and not just because of the cooking!—but be extra careful during boiling.

Step One: Dip your finger into the cocoa powder and let your partner lick it off slowly. Next, combine cocoa, sugar, and salt in a large pot (3 qt.). Add milk gradually, mixing thoroughly.

Step Two: While your partner nips and kisses your neck, bring the mixture to a boil, stirring constantly (or at least when you remember to between kisses). Turn heat to medium, continue to boil, stirring often, until it reaches 236 degrees F (soft ball stage)—about 45 to 60 minutes of exquisite foreplay. Every few minutes, change places with your partner and kiss his or her neck, while letting your hands roam freely. (The person nearest to the stove should wear a sexy apron to protect against splattering.)

Step Three: Carefully remove pan from heat, add butter and vanilla, stir. Cool fudge to 110 degrees F (about 20 minutes, giving you time to kiss a little lower than the neck).

Step Four: Take turns beating (the fudge, not each other!) energetically by hand until fudge thickens and loses some of its gloss — about 10 minutes. (The person not beating the fudge should find something else creative to do with their hands.) Quickly spread fudge in a greased 8"x8"x2" glass dish. Cool before cutting. To test if fudge is cool, put a dab on the inside of your partner's thigh and slowly lick it off, savoring every last bit.

Feed each other a small piece of fudge before engaging in other sensuous activities.

About the author:

Before plunging wholeheartedly into writing erotic romance, Bella got a BA in Economics at Stanford University, worked as a marketing director, and strutted hundreds of stages as a rock star. She currently lives in Northern California with her fabulous husband, who thinks his wife is cooler than his friends' wives, because she writes erotic romance.

Bella welcomes mail from readers. You can write to her c/o Ellora's Cave Publishing at 1056 Home Ave. Akron, Oh. 44310-3502.

Also by Bella Andre:

Passion and Ecstasy
Crown Jewels
Shooting Stars

Valentine Wishes

Mlyn Hurn

Chapter One

"National Suck-Up Day!" Valentina Vale spoke softly and then she took a sip of her gourmet coffee. The handsome gray-haired man seated beside her at the small table in the trendy coffee shop coughed in surprise at her words. As she watched, he wiped his mouth with his napkin. "And before you ask, Mark, no, I'm not kidding. That is exactly what her ex-fiancé called Valentine's Day."

Mark Magnuson shook his head in disbelief. "And that is the excuse he used to avoid buying your daughter a present?"

"Yes. This started with Vicky's first real boyfriend in high school. I thought he was a schmuck, but Victoria seemed to find something attractive in him. What that was I'll never understand! Not a single one of Vicky's suitors had an ounce of true romance in them. I'm not saying my daughter's had a slew of men in her life, but her ex-fiancé…well, he was the worst—the straw that broke the camel's back, so to speak." Valentina reached out and covered Mark's hand with hers.

"That's one of the reasons I'm anxious to have her participate in the fashion show. I want her to believe in love and romance once again. She has gone on a few dates since moving away, so it isn't that she hates men. Quite honestly I know that I am probably being the overprotective mother. Most likely it's because of my happiness and now I want my daughter to have the same. And I know she is going to love you, Mark."

"I'm looking forward to finally meeting your elusive daughter, darling."

"I know, Mark. She hates this time of the year. I think she refuses to go anywhere until Valentine's Day is finally over. Her life is just home and her job, which is done almost entirely from her apartment for now. Her quiet period is the break between Valentine's Days and Easter." Valentina shrugged, shaking her head.

Mark put his hand over hers and squeezed gently. "It sounds like this jerk really did a number on your daughter. They weren't married, right?"

"No, luckily she wasn't that foolish. He did ask her, though, several times. I think the problem goes much deeper than just this last man. In high school, she dated some jock on the football team. He was of the opinion that he was popular enough that he didn't need to buy a girl any gifts. I'm beginning to fear that perhaps Vicky just has terrible taste in men — unlike me, of course."

Valentina leaned toward her new husband and kissed him lightly. "I love you, Mark Magnuson. I am so glad that I knocked you down in Venice."

Mark laughed and nodded his head. "Me, too, my love. I wish Vicky could have come to the wedding."

"I know. I feel unmotherly in agreeing with you, Mark, because I wish she had come as well. She has decided that she doesn't want to fly ever again."

"I can understand her fears, though, Valentina. After all, she was on one of the planes that were in the air the morning of September eleventh. A lot of people are still suffering from post-traumatic stress disorder in one way or another."

"And if we'd delayed the wedding long enough for her to drive back to New York City from California then she would have come. I considered waiting, except you were leaving again and I wanted to travel with you. I'm just so glad that your son took over the financial end of my business. I don't know if he realizes how much he has relieved my stress and freed my creative spirit once again."

"Nothing in this world pleases Kirk more than having more money to worry over."

"Still, Mark, there was nothing in our loan papers that suggested his stepping in to manage everything on such a personal level." Valentina took a sip of her coffee and then glanced at her watch. "Oh dear! I've got to scoot, darling! I'm supposed to be meeting Vicky at the store for her fitting. Somehow I just know it is going to be painful."

"What will be painful, darling?"

"Just the whole returning home thing, Mark. She'll be faced with her ex-fiancé at the store—"

"What? Who?"

"I'm sorry, darling. I should have told you sooner. Her fiancé was Nick Ingles. They worked together, which I guess is how they got together. Only after they started dating did Nick share his views on romance and holidays."

"Why would a guy down on romance go into designing wedding dresses?"

Valentina laughed as she shook her head negatively. "I think it was a case of being so damned good at something that he got steered in this direction. Anyway, he was just the last straw for Vicky. There were only a few guys she dated before Nick, but each one seemed to have the same mind-set."

"Has she been dating since she moved there?"

"She says yes, but I doubt it. I think she decided to become a new kind of hermit."

"Hmm. Are you sure she doesn't hate men? Maybe all the while this was leading to one of those life-altering changes kind of thing." Mark shrugged his shoulders, his embarrassment at even broaching the subject apparent on his face and in his demeanor.

"Unless things changed dramatically, no. Whenever we'd go shopping and see an attractive, strapping young stud I would see her looking. Vicky always denied it, saying it was the artist in her that appreciates his good bone structure. But I would get her by asking what bone structure lies in his ass!"

Mark laughed out loud. Picking up his wife's hand, he pressed his lips to her fingers.

"I just wish that something wonderful would happen for her," Valentina murmured.

"Perhaps she will have surprised you and developed a whole new attitude regarding Valentine's Day and love."

Valentina stood and hugged her handsome new husband. "I am always hopeful. We'll see you for dinner at the restaurant. Kirk knows the time and place, right?"

"Yes, darling. And I'll call him again to verify things. Stop worrying!"

* * * * *

Victoria Vale cursed the fates above once again. Of course she loved her mother and would do anything for her, like give her a kidney or something like that. But appearing in a Valentine's Day fashion show was pushing her buttons, and her nerves were wearing thin.

The drive had been uneventful, even in a rental car. At least it was only one way, and she was going home on the train. The only problem had been driving in the city, to the rental office. She'd forgotten how much she liked, but also disliked the city. The quiet life she lived in California suited her so much better than this frantic-paced urban jungle. Still, there were things in the city that she truly did like. Taking a deep breath, she stepped out of the elevator and onto the floor where her mother's office was located. Her secretary, Denise, wasn't at her desk, so she walked straight into her mother's office.

For the first couple of moments everything looked normal. White lace, silk and satin were scattered nearly everywhere in the room. Several mannequins were in different stages of undress. White shoes half in and half out of their boxes occupied one corner. In another corner were at least three torso-only mannequins, displaying very sexy lingerie. Vicky felt her eyes widen in shock as she saw how skimpy and exotic some of the pieces of underwear appeared to be. She'd never seen lingerie or shoes in her mother's office before. Surely her mother wasn't expanding her business!

"You're late! Strip off quickly because the fitter will be here in a few minutes."

Vicky turned to where the voice was coming from. A tall, dark-haired man was standing behind her mother's desk, going through some papers in his hands. He wasn't even looking at her. Okay, she thought, reminding herself to be patient, after all he was only a man.

"Excuse me…" Vicky spoke softly to get his attention.

Suddenly the man looked up and she saw that he was wearing wire-rimmed glasses so she couldn't really see his eye color. But the look on his face didn't appear in the least bit welcoming. His voice and words reinforced her premonition exactly.

"Good God! You're all wrong! Denise!" he yelled as he set the papers down on the desk.

"She's not at her desk."

"Then who told you to come in here?" The man was coming around the desk. It was impossible for Vicky not to stare at his tall, fit body, which was revealed by the jeans and white T-shirt he was wearing. Perhaps her mother had hired a personal assistant. This one would certainly put a stir into the hearts of the women who worked here!

"No one told me to come in. I just walked in," Vicky added, as if that would help explain things.

"Do I need to call security to get you to leave?"

What nerve! Vicky didn't like this new assistant of her mother's. Sure, he was gorgeous to look at, but looks were not important, as she'd learned the hard way…twice! Clearing her throat, she shook her head and replied.

"I always walk in without waiting." Vicky instinctively took a combatant stance she'd learned in her Tai Kwan Do class. She kept her hands down, letting her purse slide off her shoulder. "And who are you, anyway?"

"Not that it's any of your business, but I am Kirk Magnuson."

* * * * *

Kirk paused a few feet from the feisty, dark auburn-haired woman. Something about her seemed familiar, but he couldn't decide what it was. She was too plump to be a model, unless she was one of the plus-size models for the line expansion Valentina was undertaking with the loan she'd gotten from his father. He still had trouble calling her "mother" or even thinking of her as his stepmother.

Folding his arms across his chest, he slowly let his eyes move over the woman's form. She was wearing jeans—as he was—but hers were tight and clung to all her rounded curves. Her waist nipped in and a very impressive bosom pushed out her T-shirt. As his gaze moved upward, he noted her full lips, high cheekbones, bright blue eyes and smooth, peach-tinted skin. With her hair in a knot he could only guess that it reached her shoulders.

"Turn around," he told her in a commanding tone. As she turned, she kept watching him over her shoulder. Kirk let his eyes move down and take in the nicely rounded ass cupped by her tight jeans. Damn! She might not be a model, but she was hot! He was stunned to realize he was aroused. Abruptly he turned and stormed back to the desk. The last thing he needed in his life was a woman!

At the desk he pulled the chair out and sat down. Picking up the phone, he pressed the button for his secretary. "Denise, please bring me the lists with the models' names, agents and fees."

Less than a minute later, his office door opened and his blond secretary came in. Technically she was still Valentina's secretary, but once Valentina's office was moved to the design center, Denise would become Kirk's personal assistant. She'd only taken a few steps when she saw the woman. Instead of continuing toward him, she cried out.

"Vicky! Oh my God! It's so good to see you!"

Kirk watched in disbelief as the two women hugged. Then it dawned on him what Denise had called the other woman…Vicky. This had to be Valentina's daughter from California. That's why she had been so comfortable and walked in without even knocking. She'd lost weight and with her hair up, she looked different than the photograph Valentina carried.

Slowly he leaned back, clasping his fingers, his forearms resting on the wooden arms of his chair. So this was his elusive stepsister who was too scared to fly home for her mother's first and hopefully only wedding. He wasn't as inclined toward sympathy and understanding as Valentina and his father had been.

"I can't believe Valentina got you to agree to be in the fashion show, Vicky," Denise said with a grin, walking toward the desk and giving him the file he'd requested. And unlike her usual respectful attitude regarding her future boss, she immediately turned toward Vicky once again.

"Guilt. Like most Catholic mothers, she wields it like a master."

"Well, I know you'll do a fantastic job. Maybe we could have lunch while you're here and catch up on our lives."

"That sounds super, Denise. Once I get my schedule from Mom we can find a date."

A few seconds later Denise closed the door behind her, leaving them alone. Kirk came to his feet once again, circling the desk. From the look on her face, he was pretty sure she had not yet made the connection between his name and her mother's new husband. That alone was rather insulting. Obviously she cared so little for her mother's new husband that she wasn't used to Valentina's equally new last name. Granted, she was still Valentina Vale professionally, but with family and friends, she was Mrs. Mark Magnuson.

"So you are the famous Vicky Vale." His voice was terse and even a little condescending. Sure, he was attracted to her, but none of that should matter anymore.

"I am not famous," she replied, taking a step backwards to put a little more space between them. "I'm just the owner's daughter. Are you my mother's new assistant?"

Kirk grinned, seeing how she'd retreated from him. Obviously he was either intimidating her or setting her on edge. Either option suited him at the moment.

"Sort of, I guess. I manage all the financial sides of the business." Vicky retreated backwards another step.

"What's with the shoes and the lingerie? Is she expanding or something? I thought she was going to cut back."

"As many fashion houses have discovered, you need a profitable bridge-line to carry the haute couture successfully."

"What is a bridge…line?"

Vicky's frown and lack of knowledge made him feel good, which he argued in his head was silly, and he was starting to think his feelings were beginning to resemble sibling rivalry! Good God! How could he go from successful businessman to feeling like a randy teenager who was jealous of his stepsister? He took a deep breath before he replied. He needed to stomp these feelings into the ground.

"It's a profitable, lower-priced line of designs, such as Ralph Lauren's Polo and Calvin Klein's CK."

Vicky shook her head and crossed her arms. Kirk immediately noticed how that pushed her full breasts into prominence. Deliberately he attempted to concentrate on the conversation.

Vicky spoke slowly. "You mean she is franchising and selling her name?"

"That sounds rather stuck-up, don't you think?" he said. From the tone in her voice or perhaps it was the look on her face, it seemed easy for him to make that assumption.

"How dare you? You don't know me at all, or my mother, either, for that matter. She's always stuck to her guns and never sold out."

"Times change and you haven't been out here to help her, or really know what is going on with the business."

Vicky took a step closer. "And I suppose you have?" Suddenly she poked him in the middle of his chest with her finger.

"It's been almost two years since you last came here," Kirk reminded her callously. For some reason he wanted to rub her the wrong way. He wanted to make her lose her temper so he could see if it rose slowly or went off like a firecracker.

Vicky poked him again, stepping a bit closer. Kirk could see the fire in her eyes building slowly. "I imagine you thought that you were going to sneak in and trick my mother into marrying you, huh? Instead she goes off to Venice and marries somebody else. That leaves you as the lowly assistant."

"That's one way to look at my position," Kirk replied. And even though it was unnecessary, he crossed his arms and let the corner of his mouth turn up in a semblance of a knowing smile.

"Maybe I'll talk to my mother and have her fire you!" She jabbed him with her finger again.

Kirk shook his head side to side. "That wouldn't be wise. I'd have a good wrongful dismissal lawsuit for sure. Last thing the new bride needs is a nasty court case."

"God! You really are a—"

"Darling! When did you get here?"

Valentina Vale ran across the distance and hugged her daughter tightly. "Have you been to my old apartment yet? You can stay there, or you can come and stay with Mark and me. We have plenty of room in his townhouse. I know you'll love it there. And we're all having dinner tonight."

"Mother! Take a breath!"

"I see you two have already met. I had hoped to get here in time to introduce you, but now that you've gotten to know each other we can jump right in." Valentina tossed her purse aside. "I've arranged to have the rest of this stuff moved out of here tomorrow morning, Kirk. I think you will be much more comfortable in here once I'm gone."

Kirk had been watching his stepsister, so he caught the look that crossed her face as her mother spoke. He was still pretty sure that Vicky had not caught on to just who he really was yet. Deciding to irritate her just a little bit more before she found out the whole truth, he put his arm around Valentina's shoulders and kissed her cheek.

"I'll miss seeing your lovely face." Kirk spoke loud enough for Vicky to hear even as he hugged Valentina close. He saw the fire flare in the younger woman's eyes as her eyelids opened wider in disbelief and her mouth formed a soundless "o." This was almost too much fun. Kirk pushed away the niggling bit of conscience that wanted to question why he was really so intent on irritating his stepsister instead of trying to build a sibling relationship. He opened his mouth to explain, but Valentina stepped away and grabbed her daughter's hand.

"I'm stealing Vicky away, Kirk. We have lots to get done and not much time to accomplish it." She retrieved her purse and, tugging her daughter's hand, pulled Vicky behind her. At the door, Valentina waved and called back over her shoulder. "See you later, dear."

Chapter Two

Vicky trailed behind her mother the rest of the day. Everywhere they went people she knew greeted her warmly. Nearly every place her mother stopped appeared to be undergoing some kind of reconstruction or remodeling to some degree. The design area was more than the usual studio one might expect.

The lighting was so perfect that Vicky confessed to her mother. "I'm jealous of this studio, Mother. This lighting is fabulous. In fact, the whole studio is like a dream for any artist."

"I'd be delighted to have you come back, Victoria."

"I know, Mother. But I'm doing well with my new job. And it isn't making me quite as crazy anymore."

Valentina sat down at one of the design tables. "I think it's terrible, though, that they won't move you to another day."

Vicky smiled at her mother. "It's my fault that I happened to be the best Valentine's Day artist they've ever had for their greeting card line. Just as it's my fault that I can't stand the holiday. Good old National Suck-Up Day!"

Vicky walked over to look out the window. It always impressed her when she saw how much her mother had achieved, despite being an unwed mother-to-be at nineteen. Whereas Vicky herself had every advantage money could buy, she also had two defunct relationships, and was now doing something she really didn't love, driven from her job by her last relationship. She was almost pathetic, she decided in a moment of self-pity. All she needed now was a carton of Ben and Jerry's ice cream to top it all off.

"It's not your fault, Vicky. It's those two losers you had as boyfriends. The first one was too cheap to buy you a present on any special day and the second called it 'National Suck-Up Day.' My God, it's a miracle that you don't hate men. Uhm, you don't hate men, do you, dear?"

Vicky laughed as she shook her head. "No, Mother, I still find the opposite sex attractive." No sooner did the words leave her mouth then a vision popped into her head. It was the face of the man she'd just met in her mother's office. Immediately she could feel her heartbeat increasing, which only made her more irritated. Shaking her head again, perhaps to remove his face from her mind, Vicky crossed to stand by the table.

"First semi-attractive man to ask me and I'll go on a date with him. I haven't sworn off men, Mother." Bending forward, she rested her forearms on the table. "Working from my apartment, I just don't have that much contact."

"Couldn't you move back home then? You could just as easily send them your work from here."

Vicky looked away from her mother's pleading gaze. Lately she had been thinking the exact same thing.

"I think that sounds like a perfect idea!"

Vicky turned in surprise at hearing that voice. Her eyes told her that her ears had heard correctly—the voice did indeed belong to her last boyfriend, or fiancé, according to him. He looked just the same as he had when Vicky had said "enough" and run away. His blond hair was sun-streaked, though not naturally, and his perfect tan was achieved through a tanning salon. He was dressed to show off his physique, and she was sure he still had women falling all over him.

"Hello, Nick."

* * * * *

Halfway across the room, Kirk stopped abruptly as he saw Nick Ingles hugging Vicky. Stepping back quickly, he watched surreptitiously as Nick turned her slightly during the hug, managing to slide one hand down to cup that sweet ass he'd been admiring earlier. The surge of jealousy shocked him and he turned abruptly and stormed back up to his office. He'd wait to discuss this issue with Valentina later.

He sat waiting for thirty minutes for Vicky to return. Every time he realized that he had been waiting and watching the clock on his wall, he'd angrily get busy doing something. Of course, each time the distraction was only for a few minutes and then he was thinking about her once again. Looking at the purse Vicky had left behind, Kirk replayed in his head what he wanted to say to this impertinent little miss.

Even before he'd met her, he acknowledged that he had some pretty definite preconceptions about a daughter who didn't bother coming to her mother's wedding. It didn't matter that Valentina had told him many times that she didn't hold this against her darling daughter and once he met her, he'd see how lovely and endearing she truly was. Kirk certainly agreed she was lovely — like a lush, fully developed rose. But her temperament was something he wasn't quite so sure of.

Suddenly the door of his office opened. Swinging his chair around, he watched as Vicky walked toward him. He didn't resist the urge to let his gaze roam down her luscious body and then slowly back up. With a half-smile, he decided that Vicky Vale was like candy for the eyes. When his gaze landed on hers though, he quickly saw that she was not amused by his slow and deliberate perusal. He spoke quickly, not wanting to reveal his thoughts or the hard-on that seemed to be intermittently plaguing him since her arrival.

"Leaving so soon?" he asked, watching as she picked her purse up from where he'd placed it on the corner of his desk.

"I forgot my purse, and no, I'm not leaving just yet. I'm going to spend some time down in design."

"Staying here will only distract your mother from her work." Kirk paused as he realized how ridiculous he was starting to sound.

"I don't see that this is any business of yours, since you work for her, but I am going to help Nick with a problem he's having."

Thinking about Vicky with Nick angered him for reasons he wasn't ready to think about just yet, so he pushed them away. "How can a greeting card artist help a clothes designer?"

Vicky didn't reply right away and Kirk saw the answering flash of irritation and anger on her face. He was pretty sure that he saw her struggle to control her responses also. A moment later she swung her purse so the long strap hung over her shoulder. She then rested her hands on her hips, shifting so that one hip was cocked sideways. Vicky appeared to be ready to do battle, in his opinion.

"Look—" Vicky spoke just the one word and then shook her head. "Please call my mother if you doubt my abilities." She turned on her heel and stormed out of his office.

* * * * *

Vicky entered her mother's apartment a few hours later, setting her two suitcases on the floor. She kicked the door shut behind her as she juggled the keys, her purse and the long dress bag her mother had sent her home with. Slowly she walked into the living room, unconsciously looking for changes since she'd lived there. Like a magnet, she was drawn to the windows that overlooked the park below. Speaking out loud, her thoughts spilled out.

"I can't believe she gave up this place to move anywhere else! Where could this Mark guy live that would be better than this?"

"Perhaps Valentina just prefers living at her new husband's home."

"Eek!" Vicky screamed even as she spun around, hearing someone else in the apartment. Across the room was the man she had met earlier in her mother's office. The difference was that he was now wearing only a towel around his waist.

"I guess Valentina forgot to tell you that I was living here as well. I'm sure she figured the place was big enough for the two of us."

Vicky felt her head spinning and wanted to blame it on the lack of food. But looking at Kirk's semi-naked body she was having her doubts. That dizzy feeling and the little zinging sensations along her nerves were telling her it was an attraction, not a repulsion kind of thing. The last thing she needed, Vicky told herself sternly but silently, was to get involved with another man who worked for her mother. She reached her hand out, grabbed one of the dining room chairs and plopped down on it. In the back of her head she could hear her mother's voice reminding her not to treat antique furniture like some kind of cheap "rent to own" stuff.

Just a few seconds later, she saw that Kirk was walking toward her. Her stomach leapt into her throat and her heart began pounding. As he came closer, she took in the way his wet hair had flopped forward a little on his forehead, which only made him sexier. Instantly she knew that distance was the needed remedy here. There had not been one iota of interest shown on his part toward her and unrequited lo...her brain stumbled over the word and changed it to passion. Heck! As far as she knew, she was too full-figured for his taste, especially since he worked around skinny models all the time.

For a moment she smiled. She felt quite proud that she had not used the word f-a-t in reference to her size. It wasn't easy, but she was working on separating her self-image with her body image. Dr. Phil would be proud of her!

Meeting Kirk's eyes, she immediately realized that he was smiling back. Good God! What must he be thinking of her? Starting to stand, she reached out with one hand while resting the other on the lovely lace tablecloth. It was only natural for the linen to shift, thanks to the high gloss shine beneath it. Unfortunately, Vicky lost her balance and seemed to be falling.

Thinking about it later, it would have been better if she had fallen.

Valentine Wishes

* * * * *

Kirk had decided to sit on the chair beside Vicky. Seeing her slip, his instinctive reaction was to grab her. He was successful in catching her upper arms, and that's when he felt his towel falling off. Split-second decisions in wheeling and dealing were his specialty. This wasn't business, though. Releasing one of Vicky's arms, he tried to grab the towel. Off balance, he fell and brought Vicky down with him. He'd swear he twisted so he could cushion her landing, but the next thing he knew, he was naked and lying on top of the sexiest body he'd been attracted to in a long time.

He met her eyes a moment later and stared into the blue depths. This close to her, feeling her softly rounded belly cushioning his hips while her lush breasts pressed against his chest, there was no doubt in his mind that he was attracted to Vicky Vale, like it or not. Resistance was futile as his gaze was drawn to her full lips, which parted slightly as she breathed in and out rapidly. His usually clever and acerbic wit seemed to have deserted him all of a sudden. All he could think about was kissing her soft mouth while he curved his hand around her breast.

"You're crushing me. I know I was the softer of the two of us to land first—" Vicky spoke breathily to him.

Kirk immediately pushed upward with his hands against the floor to remove most of his weight, but it still didn't allow her to slip from beneath him. He watched her face as she pondered his half-move, wondering what she would do now. As her lower lip slipped between her teeth, he knew she was considering her options.

"I'm sorry I couldn't stop your fall," Kirk added a few seconds later.

"No, it's really my fault. I grabbed your towel…"

Vicky's voice faded away. Kirk could see the realization dawning that without his towel, he was pressed against her.

"Oh my God! You're naked!"

Kirk had to grin. "That's what usually happens when I take a shower. Have you learned of some other way than taking off all of your clothes? I'd be interested in seeing that demonstration."

Vicky pressed her hands against his shoulders. The blush that stained her cheeks also ran down her neck. Kirk wondered how far down across her chest it extended. But giving way under the steady push of her hands, he rolled away from her soft body. The towel was wrapped around his hips once again as Vicky came to her feet.

"I need to shower," she murmured as she scooted past him.

Kirk watched her pick up the dress bag. Instead of walking down the hallway, she turned to look at him. Almost as if he sensed her question, he replied quickly. "I'm in your mother's old room. Valentina wanted to keep your room just as it was when you were living here."

Vicky met his eyes for a second. "Thanks."

Kirk watched her as she almost ran away from him to her old bedroom. He turned to look out the window. This growing attraction for his stepsister was probably not a good thing. But the fall on the floor and pressing against her soft, rounded curves were giving rise to lots of sexy and amazing thoughts. Just thinking about her in the shower, letting the hot water course down across her body, was making him harder and hotter than he'd been in a very long time.

After a minute or two, he shook his head to clear his thoughts. Only problem now was that he needed a cold shower. Walking back to his room, he saw Vicky's two suitcases at the door. Shrugging, he picked up the two bags and carried them to her room. The door was only partially closed.

"Vicky? I've got your suitcases."

Kirk waited at least a minute and then he pushed the door open and walked into her room. He set both cases by the dresser. From here, he could hear the sound of the water from the shower. God! It was almost too easy to close his eyes and picture Vicky standing beneath the water spray. Was she facing the shower and letting the water hit her face before it sluiced down over her lovely, round breasts? In his imagination, Kirk saw himself stepping up close behind her. His hard cock eagerly pressed between her fleshy thighs and he lifted his hands to cup and then squeeze those lavish breasts that he was starting to daydream about on a regular basis.

Or maybe she let her head fall back so the water saturated her hair and coursed down her body. It was almost poetic, but in an erotic way, imagining her hands lifting to slick her hair away from her face. The way her breasts tilted up seemed an invitation to more than just his hands. Massaging her left boob with one hand, the other gently lifted the right for his mouth to envelope her tight nipple. Should he just circle it with his tongue or suckle it like a babe eager for sustenance?

The water stopping in the bathroom caught his attention and brought him out of his erotic daydream. Hearing the shower door open, he decided that retreat was the only real option at the moment. Vicky probably would not appreciate finding him—his cock rock hard and barely concealed by the towel — in her bedroom when she walked in a few seconds from now. Quickly, and with much regret, Kirk turned and headed toward his room.

Chapter Three

Vicky walked back into the living room, knowing that she was late. Immediately she saw that Kirk was dressed and glancing at his watch.

"I'm sorry that I'm late. I hadn't really planned on dining out tonight."

"It's fine. I doubt they're even there yet."

Nodding once, she pulled her coat around her and tucked her small, flat purse under her arm. "I'm set then. Are we taking a cab to the restaurant?"

"Yes. It's a few blocks from here and Valentina said they'd be taking the limo and would give us a ride back here afterward."

Vicky stepped past Kirk as he held the door open, and she immediately noticed the scent he was wearing. It was masculine and seemed to be mingling with her scent, lingering, and then meandering up through her senses. He had looked drop-dead gorgeous in his dark suit and light-colored tie. She tried not to stare at him, but it wasn't easy. For a few seconds, she tried focusing on Nick. That should distract her, surely.

The elevator opened up and they stepped inside. Once the doors had closed, Kirk pushed the button for the lobby and then casually pointed toward her left shoulder. As she turned, he spoke softly.

"They have two cameras in here now, so we'll have to behave ourselves."

Vicky gasped in surprise and whipped her head back around. Kirk was smiling a little. Angry, she glared at him and stared straight ahead. Damn! It didn't make her mad that he had spoken the words. She was pissed because his words had so accurately matched the thoughts going on inside her head. Like…what would Mr. Perfect do if she turned to him, slipped her hand around his neck and then kissed him hard? He'd have to use that pristine white handkerchief because she was planning on giving him a lip-lock that would leave "kiss prints" in its wake.

"We should have a cab waiting. I called down earlier and asked Charlie if he'd call one for us a few minutes ahead of time."

Vicky took a deep breath. Nervously she reached up to tuck her hair behind her right ear. There wasn't anything to push back because her hair was pinned up in a fancy forties-style hair snood her mother had bought for her. It made her look elegant, and matched the black dress she was wearing. She opened her mouth instead.

"Are you always so well-prepared?" Vicky heard the snippy remark leave her lips and wished she could immediately recall the words. If she wasn't careful, she was going to sound like an old spinster like her great-aunt Gertrude.

Kirk turned to face her, leaning against the elevator's wall. With his arms folded across his chest, he casually lifted and pressed his right foot back behind him. Vicky was intensely aware of how sexy he looked, and casual despite the expensive suit, shirt and tie he was wearing. Obviously, Kirk was one of those men who looked great in his clothes. In that classical yet relaxed pose, he could have come straight from the pages of a stylish men's magazine.

The heat covered her cheeks a second later. Popping into her thoughts was the picture of him standing before her in just the towel. There could be no argument that he had looked pretty damned good dressed in almost nothing, as well as out of the skimpy covering. Granted, she'd only gotten a brief glimpse, but the blur was impressive and left her wishing for more. During her shower it had been too easy to picture Kirk joining her. Remembering what she had been doing with her hands caused her to swallow unexpectedly and then start to cough.

Kirk's strong hand immediately pounded her back and she dropped her purse. The doors opened into the lobby, allowing her purse to bounce out before it disclosed its contents. Kirk and Charlie, the building's doorman, bent down to recover the few things that rolled out. She was ready to take a sigh of relief when she noticed that Kirk was picking up the one thing she'd forgotten was in the purse from the last time she'd used it—a condom.

It had been a night on the town with her girlfriends, and at the beginning one of them had passed out one condom a piece as she bid them, "Here's to getting lucky and being safe!"

Now, seeing the look on Kirk's face as he handed her the purse first and then the condom, told her way more information than she wanted to handle just then. Ignoring him, she greeted the older man. "Thank you, Charlie. All these years and you are still picking up my things. Thank you."

"Always a pleasure, Miss Vicky. You and your mother have always been decent to me. Treated me with respect."

Vicky smiled. She'd always liked Charlie. He'd worked here as a doorman in the evening hours and as building superintendent during the day and night hours. Two of his children were close to her age and they had played together in the basement a lot. She touched the doorman's forearm, realizing how nice it was to see people from her past. "How is your wife doing? I wrote to Mother last week asking how many grandchildren you must have by now."

Charlie laughed and escorted Vicky across the marble floor of the building's lobby. He walked out first, holding the door for her. "Not that many, Miss Vicky. Only half my kids managed to get married so far. Everybody seems to be waiting until their thirties to get married."

"This is your cab, sir," Charlie told Kirk as he opened the yellow car's rear door.

"Thank you, Charlie."

From the backseat, Vicky saw Kirk pass a twenty-dollar tip to the doorman before he climbed in beside her. As the cab pulled away from the curb, Vicky scooted a little farther away from his body heat. She admitted that was foolish, especially this time of the year. People usually huddled closer together to conserve body heat. The thought of Kirk's strong arm surrounding her shoulders made her feel quite warm and she was forced to lightly fan her face while she blew a few puffs of air upward, forcing her bangs to move slightly.

"Are you warm-blooded?" Kirk asked her a few seconds later.

Vicky knew she couldn't admit that he was the reason she felt hot! Shaking her head negatively, she realized that wasn't right so she started nodding. Admitting silently that she probably seemed like a total fool, she cleared her throat to reply. "I'm not reptilian."

Kirk surprised her by scooting across the seat and pressing up against her side. "I never would have considered you cold-blooded. Not with that fiery red hair, anyway. Besides, I touched your skin enough earlier to know how soft it is, and not a single scale in sight."

"What are you doing?" she asked quickly, even though she had a damned good idea that he was following her thoughts of conserving body heat. "And my hair is not fiery." The minute she spoke she realized that it would have been more proper for her to comment about the skin not her hair, right? Remembering the feel of his body pressed to hers so intimately was not the way to cool down! And to comment on how his skin had been would only set her up with a new daydream that would be just as impossible as the current.

"I guess it is dark enough to be called auburn, but the way your eyes spark and your temper flares, you could pass for a hot redhead."

Vicky felt the feminist in her demand a fight, but his physical warmth and the rationalization that he had called her hot sapped her brain. Of course, he probably meant just her temperament was flaming. She doubted that he would have implied she was attractive. There was no room for misconception. Her body was rounded and curvy on good days, and downright plump on others. And she worked hard not to beat herself down with the words "fat" or "worthless."

"Isn't this better?" Kirk asked a minute or so later. "Now we can keep one another warm."

Vicky nodded her head because there was no reply that wouldn't sound silly. It certainly did feel better. In fact, having Kirk's hard body pressed against her softer curves was sexy, erotic and definitely turning her on with each passing second. Every time he took a deep breath, even though her brain was telling her that she was being silly, it seemed like he moved a little closer. She wasn't imagining when he slid his arm around her shoulders.

"Not much heat in some of these cabs, huh?" he told her, smiling at her even as his hand curved over her shoulder.

Smiling back was inevitable. Kirk's smile was gorgeous, in her opinion, with near-perfect white teeth and a mouth she was seeing herself kissing every time she closed her eyes. Her lips curved up as she shook her head.

"I think they charge more if you have heat," Vicky replied. As soon as she closed her mouth, she wanted to kick herself. What a stupid thing to say! She practically accused him of being cheap. Before she could correct her previous statement, Kirk grinned at her again.

"If I'd known it was an option, I'd have checked the box on the reservation form."

Vicky laughed and she felt her body relaxing. It felt natural and right that she turned toward him somewhat on the seat. "I was just impressed that you thought ahead to have Charlie get the cab for us."

Kirk's right hand lifted and gently pulled a few strands of her hair away from her lips, which had caught in the lipstick darkening her mouth. His fingers didn't just pull the hairs free, though. Slowly she felt the cool, fleshy pads of his fingertips caress her cheek for a second or two. Then he tucked the hairs behind her ear. It was impossible to stop the shiver that coursed through her body when his skin contacted the sensitive rim of her ear. Breathing in deeply, it seemed like he started to lower his head—

"Here you go, folks!"

Kirk passed the money to the cabdriver as he scooted toward the far door. "Thanks for waiting, and for the ride."

Vicky knew that she was now going to have to scoot across the seat to exit. It was impossible to prevent her skirt sliding up to the top of her thighs, and her right thigh was completely visible to anyone who chose to look. Kirk's hand came into her view, offering to help, and she took it gratefully.

"Thank you," she murmured as she stood beside him.

"Let's head in and see if they beat us here. If not, at least we can warm up."

* * * * *

Kirk scanned the restaurant and saw that his father and new stepmother were already seated. He waved to them while waiting for Vicky to return from checking her coat and combing her hair in the ladies room. If she'd asked him, he'd have told her she looked great. She certainly had appeared kissable, desirable and amazingly fuck-able beside him in that cab. Ten seconds more on that damned backseat and he would have tested the durability of her lipstick.

"Sorry for taking so long."

"Not a problem, Vicky. They are already seated."

Vicky nodded and moved in front of him as he gestured for her to precede him. She'd only gone about two steps when he saw what her coat had so successfully concealed. The dress fit almost like skin and was backless to within an inch or so of her waist. As she walked on the three-inch heels, his eyes appreciated the gentle sway of her hips and the sexy little jiggle as each foot struck the floor. Damn! Dinner was going to be hard in more ways than one.

Just getting through the evening, watching Vicky and remembering how tempting it had been on the floor, was going to give him recurring visions and daydreams. This whole situation was "outside the box" but the truth of the matter was that he was horny as hell for his new stepsister! So in his mind, dinner would be a long, drawn out affair to suffer through.

Mark Magnuson was already standing and he greeted Vicky with a hug. "You sit next to your mother. I'm sure you two ladies still have a lot of catching up to do."

Kirk saw the flush on Vicky's cheeks as she took the chair his father was holding for her. From what he'd seen of his stepsister so far, his dad's usual friendly and casual manner would take her some getting used to. Reluctantly he took the seat opposite Vicky that was beside his father. Looking from Vicky to her mother, it was obvious that Vicky was none other than Valentina's daughter. He hoped that Vicky wouldn't be too pissed off when she realized that he was more than some guy who worked for her mother.

Chapter Four

Vicky glared at Kirk across the length of the living room. She'd held her tongue all evening, curtailing her jumbled emotions until it was just the two of them. There was no way he was going to avoid a discussion on the truth. It had all started at the restaurant. They'd only been seated at the table a few minutes when her new stepfather had patted Kirk on the back.

"Well, Vicky, how are you and your new stepbrother getting along so far? Val was hoping that with the two of you sharing her old apartment you'd have more time to get acquainted."

Vicky knew she had smiled, but from that point on she didn't remember much of anything that was said. By the time dinner ended, her cheeks hurt from forcing the smile onto her face. Inside of her, hurt and anger were boiling over. The problem, as she saw it, was that she couldn't even be sure who deserved her anger.

Her mother had not said a word about Kirk being her new stepson or Vicky's stepbrother. Kirk, for that matter, had not bothered to point out their new relationship. She was the angriest at herself for not catching on in the first place to the new family dynamics. She knew her mother's new husband had a son. It had not made sense that she'd let one of her employees move into her old apartment. Vicky told herself countless times during dinner that she was an idiot for not catching on sooner. She almost hit her forehead with the palm of her hand at missing all those clues; especially that Kirk's last name was the same as the man her mother had married. Duh, she admonished silently.

Now, back in the apartment, Kirk was watching her as he removed his suit jacket, followed by untying and then pulling the silk tie from around his neck. Tossing them both onto the sofa, he idly rolled his shirtsleeves part way up each forearm. The reason she was really pissed was because she had allowed herself to be attracted to this man. For almost eight hours he'd been starring in mini-daydreams in her mind, and each one had been getting even more erotic and electrifyingly arousing than the last. Her enforced abstinence since her break-up with Nick had not been difficult until today. Meeting Kirk had released all of her pent up sexual needs and energies, and possibly some of her long buried wishes as well.

A moment later, she realized that her gaze was glued to his hands as they started unbuttoning his shirt and it was too much for Vicky's overwrought nerves. She spun away and walked over to the windows, staring out at the blackness beyond. Soon she saw his reflection appear just a short distance behind her. Being stern and logical, she told herself to look away from his sexy body as it was mirrored in the glass. Less than two seconds later she looked at his image reproduced almost perfectly in the night-darkened window. She needed to read his thoughts, if that was even possible in her harried state.

His voice surprised her as he spoke softly. "I owe you an apology, Vicky."

"For what, Kirk, mistaking me for a tenth of a millisecond as a model? Forget about it! That happens to me all the time," she added, hoping she could joke her way out of this conversation completely and perhaps save a little bit of her dignity.

Kirk's hand came out and lightly touched her back, near the naked skin at her waistline. Vicky jumped a little, but she didn't pull away. Her brain told her to step out of touching range. Touching would not be a good idea right now, she argued on the inside. Instead she just stood there, trying to figure out if it was his fingertips or the smoother skin on the back of his hands that was gently touching her back. Her eyelids felt heavy and drifted shut, hopefully concealing her true emotions from Kirk.

"No," he told her softly. "I realized almost immediately that you did not understand who I was in your mother's office."

Vicky kept her eyes closed, savoring the warmth of his hand against her skin. He hadn't increased the touch yet, nor had he pulled away. She wasn't sure if this was a brotherly "how-ya-doin" thing or would be considered a caress between adults. It felt wonderful and she didn't want it to stop. Her conscience butted in to remind her that Kirk was her *stepbrother*. That's when his hand flattened to her flesh and she felt the full, hot imprint of his palm and every single one of his fingers. Slowly it moved sideways, edging under the fabric slightly. It was almost too easy to imagine his hand caressing its way forward and up until he held her—

Bbbbbbrrrrrriiiinnnngggggg! Bbbbrrrrrriiiiiinnnnggggg.

"Hell! Who the f…sorry. I can't imagine who'd be calling this time of the evening." Kirk moved toward the phone.

Vicky watched his retreating reflection in the glass. She couldn't hold back the regretful shuddering sigh that escaped her lips. Turning toward the room, she followed him. "It's probably my mother," she murmured as Kirk jerked the receiver off the base.

"Hello!"

Vicky cringed a little at the tone in his voice, but if she'd been the one to pick up the phone her voice would have cracked from dryness. She picked up her purse, planning to go to her room, when Kirk spoke once more. His tone was a lot softer and friendlier.

"No, Val, we were sitting in the living room talking. The meeting tomorrow morning?"

Vicky watched as Kirk turned to look at her. She couldn't read what his thoughts were but the changes on his face told her that he didn't agree with whatever it was that her mother was talking about. The conversation didn't last much longer before Kirk banged the receiver back down.

"Bad news?" Vicky asked him softly. Her earlier desire to needle him was gone. In its place was a desire to comfort him, as well as the even stronger lust to jump his bones!

* * * * *

Kirk looked at Vicky, still feeling the desire that had driven him to touch her a few minutes earlier.

"Val wants me to bring you to the meeting tomorrow morning. That's what she was calling about."

Vicky nodded, and then she asked him, "And you don't think that's a good idea?"

"I didn't say that," he told her quickly, the whole time cursing the timing of the phone call. "It's a financial meeting with the department heads."

"Well, I agree with you. I'm going to bed and you can tell my mother that I slept in." Vicky turned and walked out of the living room.

Kirk watched her undulating hips as she moved away from him. She stopped after a few feet, pausing to lift her right foot. He watched her perilous balance as she leaned over slightly to remove her shoe. She quite possibly wouldn't have lost her footing if he had not jogged the few feet and put his hands on her waist. But he surprised her enough that she did lose it, and toppled forward. Kirk tightened his hold and they stayed upright.

"Lift the other foot and I'll take that one off," he offered while still holding her waist.

A few seconds passed before she did as he suggested. He didn't resist the urge to caress her ankle before slipping the high-heeled shoe from her foot. Her balance was reestablished but Kirk didn't release his hold right away. When Vicky looked up, he no longer resisted the urge he'd been fighting since a short time after he'd met her earlier that day in his office. He covered her mouth with his, preventing whatever she'd started to say. She turned toward him as his mouth lifted briefly.

Kirk looked into her beautiful blue eyes. Without further pause, he took her lips again. His hands pulled her close to his body, holding her tightly. As he felt her fingers lightly touching his waist, he relaxed his grip to see what she would do. He realized that he'd really rushed her, and perhaps—

"We probably shouldn't do this," Vicky whispered as she pulled her mouth away from his for a few seconds.

"Why not?"

"Uhm...it's wrong."

Kirk felt Vicky's hands flattening against his chest, slowly sliding upward. The motion stopped as her fingertips encountered his hard nipples beneath the soft, fine cotton. He watched her intently, but her gaze had lowered to rest on her hands. And then he felt the tentative, but intensely arousing sensation caused by the probing of her fingertips lightly exploring his areola. When she delicately rubbed back and forth across his hard buds, a carefully suppressed groan escaped his throat. He realized that she had heard him when she repeated the touch. This time it was a rapid, flicking against each bud.

His eyes closed as he savored the increase of his ardor with each passing touch of her fingers. If his cock got much harder, he figured he would embarrass himself, which had not happened since his teen years. It was easy to wonder what it would feel like to press against her softly rounded belly. From there it was not difficult to imagine how sweet it might feel to be buried deep inside her body.

"Sweet heaven above, Vicky, you are driving me crazy!" Kirk groaned as her fingers curved inward to squeeze the muscles beneath her hands.

* * * * *

Vicky seemed to come out of her sensual fog, hearing his hoarse voice pleading for her…she wasn't sure if he wanted her to continue or stop. In fact, all she'd been concerned with was her own pleasure. The whole time she caressed his broad chest and explored his hard nipples, she'd been wondering how it would feel if her hands were resting on his warm flesh instead of the cotton of his shirt.

Lifting her head, she saw that Kirk's eyes were closed and his jaw clenched. Rising on her tiptoes, Vicky pressed her mouth to his. Ignoring all the signals that told her this was a bad idea and she really should stop, she slid her tongue along his lower lip. Before she had a chance to think about her next action, Kirk's reaction took her by surprise.

His mouth opened and their tongues met. There wasn't a battle, though. Vicky surrendered to his skill. Dimly she became aware of Kirk gently guiding and moving them down the hall into her bedroom. When they reached the side of the bed, she had already unbuttoned his shirt, which rather surprised her. His hands fell away from the fastening of her dress behind her neck. She watched his hands strip his clothes off completely. Her eyes roamed over his trim and toned physique with admiration and desire. Wetness had flooded her pussy lips and the curling heat in her gut was making her hips unconsciously move to seek out his manhood.

She forgot her dress had been unfastened in her eagerness to touch his hard cock, jutting proudly toward her. Kirk's groan of desire told her that he liked the feel of her soft hands as they grasped him. When her hands began to squeeze and pull, a shudder shook his entire body. The dim light coming from the living room revealed the slickness of pre-come oozing forth. Suddenly Vicky wanted to do something she'd never done before. She bent her knees so she could kneel before him.

Suddenly Kirk's hands grabbed her upper arms, stopping her descent abruptly. "Not yet, my sweet," he whispered through clenched teeth.

Vicky felt her arms pushed to her sides, which allowed her dress to finally fall. The black material caught for a second on her breasts, and then it fell to her waist. Since the dress had a built-in bra, she was now naked above it. She tried to lift her hands to conceal her large bosoms, but Kirk's hands held her tight.

"Is there some kind of fastening I missed?"

"In the back—"

In less than three seconds he released the hooks and slid the zipper down. With minimal encouragement, her dress eased over her hips and dropped to her feet. Standing nervously in just her pantyhose, Vicky wondered if Kirk was seeing what she saw in her mirror every day. She was a plump, size fourteen gal who'd unfortunately inherited her grandmother's impressive breasts. For most of her life she'd worn loose tops to disguise her rapid growth, and she was still uncomfortable in the kind of dress she'd worn tonight.

"All throughout dinner I kept wondering what you had on under that damned dress," Kirk whispered to her as his hands caressed their way up her arms. When he reached her shoulders, they curved up over her neck to cup her face. One thumb lightly caressed her lower lip for a second or two. Then he lowered his head and kissed her mouth once more.

The kiss was lighter this time, gentler. Lips met for a few moments and then slipped away again. He placed a kiss on each cheekbone before he returned to her mouth. This time his tongue teased her lips apart. Vicky expected an onslaught but instead he continued to tantalize her lips and tongue, which only increased her torment. Dimly she realized that Kirk was seducing her with his gentleness. He used slow, deliberate caresses, pausing every so often to change the pace. She was already so hot that she was ready to flop on the bed and yell, "Fuck me!"

"Soon, my sweet. Very soon."

Kirk's voice made her aware that she'd spoken out loud. She felt her face flush hotly in embarrassment. Her hands lifted to cross over her chest. The smile on his face unnerved her, especially when he made no effort to lower her protective and concealing hands.

"I'm going to peel these pantyhose down."

Vicky held her breath as she felt his thumbs catch under the elastic band. He pulled the elastic out and began easing them over her hips. Partway over her belly, he paused.

"Turn and face the other way, please."

She must have revealed her doubt at his request because he added quickly, "It's all right. I'd like to fulfill a fantasy I've had since you walked into my office earlier today."

Nodding her head, Vicky turned away from Kirk. Maybe she'd read him wrong and he was interested in some kinky kind of sex. Other than hating Valentine's Day, the only two males in her life had been straightforward. Since she'd only slept with Nick, and made out with the other one, her experience of the unusual was nil.

Taking a deep breath, she felt Kirk easing her hose down past her hips, her thighs and finally they dropped to her feet. Without waiting to be asked, she stepped free of the discarded clothing. Then she felt his warmth as Kirk moved close behind her. His breath danced across her right shoulder a second before the searing heat of his flesh met hers. Her gasp of surprise was audible.

"Ooh!"

Both of Kirk's hands curved around her upper arms. There was no mistaking the hot, hard flesh that was now pressed between her butt cheeks. Shifting from one foot to the other, she slightly parted her legs. Without a pause, Kirk's cock slid closer to his goal. When she heard his low, guttural moan of desire, Vicky tilted her hips and rubbed back, against his groin.

"God, Vicky!"

His hands slid down and cupped her hips. She responded quickly by flexing her pelvis forward and back several times. The hard rod slid between her wet lips. It surprised her how sexy and desirable she was feeling. From somewhere inside herself, she found the courage to be bold. With a deep breath, she took a step forward and knelt on the bed. Slowly, she bent over and rested on her forearms on the sheets. Closing her eyes, not even sure if this was the right position, she waited.

Chapter Five

Kirk couldn't speak. He was stunned by what Vicky was offering, if he understood her correctly. Several of his fantasies today had featured her in this position and one of them had involved his desk. Stepping close to the bed, he lifted his hands and placed them on her lower back. He felt the startled surprise that jumped through Vicky's exposed body. It wasn't too late. He could stop—

His hands moved down her sides and then inward to cup her cheeks. The groan that came from his gut sounded loud to him, but he could not take his hands away from her luscious, round body. Pressing close to her rounded bottom, he pushed his cock between her upper thighs and wet, pink pussy lips. His right hand slid around her body and down. Moving his fingers around, he didn't feel her pubic hair. Delving further, he continued wiggling his fingers and eased onto her clitoris.

"Ooh, my God!" Vicky cried out in response.

Kirk held her tightly, wrapping his free arm around her waist and pressing their bodies tightly together. Vicky flexed her hips and Kirk felt his cock pushing beyond her soft, puffy flesh. Suddenly he realized that he didn't have a condom in his pants pocket. Then he saw the purse she tossed onto the bed. Leaning more fully across her, which pushed him deeper inside, Kirk grabbed the purse. Dumping the contents, he grabbed the condom. He was surprised that he fumbled getting it on.

Sheesh! He was acting like an excited teen and this was his first time ever! His fingers had turned into nearly useless nubs as he tried to tear the package open. Suddenly the condom flew out. He snatched it mid-flight before it went too far, and then Kirk paused to take a deep breath or he knew the whole thing was going to end right there.

Finally, he pressed close against her again. Eagerly he ran his hands down her back, all around her ass and then resumed his earlier position. Her body responded immediately to his clever fingers on her clit.

"Oh…oh…God!" Vicky moaned and loudly called out in response.

Kirk pressed with his hands, tilting her pelvis to the right position. His thrust was straight and true. His cock was now buried to the hilt and neither one of them moved for several long moments. When he felt Vicky tilt her pelvis and squeeze her muscles, he knew she was ready. Immediately he began tickling, teasing and working her sensitive nub. As she wiggled and pushed back against him, Kirk increased the attention to her stimulated, super-sensitive clit.

"There…yes!" she whispered as he touched one place in particular.

He shifted his finger. Kirk increased his tempo, repeating the same movement that had evoked her response. Her hips were doing most of the thrusting action until she stiffened for a second, and then her orgasm came crashing over her. Shifting both his hands to her waist, he held her steady as her body shivered and shook in reaction. The pull he felt around his cock couldn't be denied any longer. Holding her firmly, he started thrusting against her plump bottom, loving each and every time he felt her cunt muscles dragging along his rod as he withdrew. And with each push forward, he heard the slap of his balls against her bald pussy.

It was the anticipatory thought of soon seeing her plump, bald pussy that collapsed the last of his control. His grip tightened on her waist and he thrust hard into her sweet flesh. His climax came fast and hard. His hips jerked forward several times as his body shot forth his seed.

As Kirk released her waist, Vicky collapsed onto the bed. Quickly disposing of the used condom, he came down, lying next to her. Using his closest hand, he gently pushed the hair back that covered her face. Her eyes opened as he ran his index finger down the bridge of her nose. As hard as he tried, he couldn't tell what she might be thinking from the placid look on her face.

* * * * *

Vicky stared at Kirk's handsome face. Her body was still in shock from the wild orgasmic release she'd experienced at his unbelievably clever hands and body. Her fantasies were tame in comparison to the real thing. Her breathing slowed somewhat as she realized that she needed to roll onto her side or back to be comfortable.

"I need to turn over, so I might as well get under the covers."

"Then let's go get into my bed. It's bigger and we'll be more comfy in there."

Vicky wasn't sure how to take Kirk's suggestion. He was already coming to his feet, though, and holding his hand out to offer her help getting off the bed. Unable to think of anything to say that would allow her to cover up, she turned and reached up to accept. Looking down at her feet to avoid seeing Kirk's expression as he saw her body from the front, she started toward the door. It wasn't until they reached his darkened bedroom that she realized that she had ended up leading him.

Kirk turned on the lights as he walked into the room. He stepped around her and turned on a lamp beside the bed. Flipping back the covers, he smiled.

"I usually sleep on this side, but if you prefer it—"

Vicky shook her head, glancing up as Kirk moved past her again. This time he turned the overhead light out. When she started toward the far side, Kirk's voice stopped her.

"Get in on my side. I'm turning on the bathroom light in case you wake up during the night."

Vicky quickly crawled into the bed and scooted over to the far side. As Kirk came back, she was lying supine and had the blankets pulled up to her chin. But her eyes moved down over his broad chest, past his waist, and stopped upon reaching his groin. She didn't realize she was staring until he spoke as he flicked the lamp off.

"Staring like that has a strange effect on me." Kirk slid into the king-size bed. In the dim light, Vicky saw him roll onto his side, facing her. "And while there is nothing I'd like better than to spend most of tonight making love with you, we have to be at the damned meeting in the morning."

Vicky flushed at his words. The thought of doing more fun things with him had been going through the back of her mind as well. Hearing him express their sex act as making love caused her to get those nervous little butterflies in her stomach. Suddenly, thousands of wings were beating madly inside her. She watched as Kirk turned back over and began setting the bedside clock.

Taking a deep breath, she told herself to calm down. It was time to sleep.

She rolled onto her side, away from him, because this was how she usually slept. Closing her eyes, she told herself that this was no big deal. Lots of people stayed the night to sleep after sex. The truth of the matter was that she'd never shared a bed with anyone. Well, that wasn't completely true. Occasionally she would come into her mother's room as a child late at night seeking comfort. Her mother always let Vicky burrow next to her, while she told her daughter how much she loved her. Of course, Vicky recalled with a small smile, her mother would often tell an extra bedtime story as well.

The bed shifted and she felt Kirk's heat coming toward her. His hand lightly touched her hip as he settled in close behind her.

"Spoon fashion! I'm glad you thought of it, sweetheart."

Vicky's eyes opened wide as Kirk nestled in tightly behind her. It was hard to be aware of all the sensations at once. She felt his breath on her neck and shoulder as he lifted her hair and draped it forward. His hand lightly caressed its way down the slightly curved line of her back to her waist. It was nearly overwhelming as the heat from his groin pressed firmly against her bottom. With his arm draping forward, across her hip, it brought his chest in contact with her back.

Lying there in the darkness, Vicky was so keyed up that she couldn't be wound any tighter. But then Kirk slowly eased his hand away from her waist. Her breath caught in her chest as his hand touched the bottom curve of her breast. That nipple was already pearled up tight in anticipation of being discovered.

It didn't have long to wait. Kirk's fingers lightly rubbed the underside for a few seconds. But that wasn't his goal. Moving purposefully, his hand inched upward. Vicky expected him to cup her breast and begin squeezing. That had been the approach she'd experienced in the past. Instead, Kirk used just one finger to find her taut nipple. Vicky couldn't keep from stiffening her spine in surprise at this light and questing exploration.

Breathing quite shallowly, she felt his finger barely touch the tip. Next he circled the half-inch extension of puckered flesh by circling around it several times. What Vicky didn't expect was to hear Kirk's voice or feel the rumble in his chest as he spoke.

"You have beautiful breasts."

Nervous, and surprised by what Kirk had said, she spoke quickly. "I used to sleep in here with my mother."

Immediately the sensual caress paused. Vicky got the distinct sense that her nipple was becoming harder and longer, as if it was trying to eliminate the short gap between itself and Kirk's seductive caress.

"I changed the bed," he replied a few moments later, and then he slowly resumed the erotic touch.

Vicky closed her eyes in the near darkness. It didn't make her happy when she admitted that the sense of relaxation was relief because Kirk had resumed his seductive caress once again. She felt the rumble in his chest as he started to speak.

"Almost from the first second I saw you, Vicky, I began fantasizing about your breasts."

"Ooh!" she gasped, unable to stop the surprised utterance.

"Given more time, I'd be happy to enact a few of the fantasies out with you, and if you'd like, I'd be equally pleased to help you with yours. Perhaps I'll dedicate one entire day to worshipping these lovely globes of your womanhood." Kirk's hand enclosed her right breast and just held the firm flesh for a few seconds before gently squeezing it. "Let's see…breakfast in bed. You'll sit up, propped by the pillows, with the sheet and blankets pooled about your waist. But your luscious body will be naked from there up."

Vicky gasped, breathing in deeply. She felt her breast fill his hand, which was now just holding her.

"I will feed you breakfast."

"You've already eaten." Vicky forced the words past her dry throat.

"No. My reward for making you breakfast is something special. I brought in strawberry jam and I'm going to spread it all over your nipples. Then I will take my time in licking it off. First a few long, slow strokes of my tongue. Followed by a good, tight sucking to make sure I miss nothing."

Vicky groaned softly as she felt the response deep down in her body. Her hips reacted instinctively by tilting and wiggling. His statement formed an exciting word picture in her mind. A moment later she felt his hand tightening around her breast, massaging gently, but with more purpose than earlier.

"Lunch will be in the kitchen, I think. We will have fresh fruit, which we will feed to one another."

Vicky was stunned as she heard her voice asking him a question. It seemed her body was taking over from her usually controlling brain!

"Naked?"

Kirk growled low in his throat and pressed a kiss to her shoulder. "I think that sounds best. You will sit on the table."

"And where will you be?"

"I'll start with feeding you and standing between your thighs. But I'm going to kiss my way down your body until you lie flat on your back, legs wide open. Then I will sit down and feast upon the treat that awaits me."

Vicky suddenly realized that Kirk's hand had moved down her body as he spoke. He was lifting her uppermost thigh, pushing it upward, toward her stomach. She felt his body shift and his hand was now on her lower leg, the inner thigh. It moved upward and without delay, his fingers delved between her pussy lips. The touch upon her clit made her jerk in surprised and uncontrollable reaction.

Each seductive movement of his finger caused an answering response in her body. Vicky lost track of how long Kirk continued to manipulate her sensitized flesh before she heard him whisper into her ear.

"Turn over and face me."

Unable to resist the lure of his touch and the promise his words offered, she shifted onto her back. As she lifted her eyelids, the light beside the bed came on once again. Closing them quickly to block the brightness out, she heard a drawer open. It was only when she felt Kirk's hand at her waist did she realize that the covers had dropped down that far. With one flip of his hand, she was completely naked, bathed in the dim light.

"Open your eyes, Vicky. Please."

As she complied, she saw him above her, resting on his bent elbow. His hair was slightly tousled and fell onto his forehead. Once again she was struck by how sexy and handsome he was.

"Just laying here on the bed with you, talking about your breasts…and I'm all ready to go again, looking at your beautiful body." His hand touched her stomach, gently pressing it flat. "I'm wondering which one of us is going to call in sick so we can skip the meeting."

Vicky gasped and coughed in surprise at his suggestion. The truth was that she wanted to repeat what they'd done earlier. And she wanted to do it again and again and again—

"I'm almost never sick," she whispered in reply.

Kirk shrugged, grinning. "Well I went through a whole list of illnesses in high school to skip out of school. I'll pick a good one that requires some tender, extra close nursing care."

His hand slid up her stomach, between her breasts and lightly curved around her chin. He lowered his mouth and kissed her gently at first. When his tongue ventured forth, it was met by Vicky's, and eagerly welcomed. Deepening the kiss, he slipped his hand down and over her farthest breast. He swallowed her moan as he massaged her full soft flesh.

Vicky felt like she was drowning under the onslaught of sensuality. His mouth was masterful; he kissed her like no one ever had before, not even in her wildest fantasies or dreams. The large, strong hand molded her breast and squeezed it gently then firmly, alternating its rhythm, keeping her on the edge of what was to happen next. Her back bowed to press her captured breast more deeply into his grasp. Right then it felt as if no release could be possible, and that made her happy.

But seconds, or perhaps it was minutes later, her breast was exposed to the air as his hand arrowed straight and true down her stomach. When he cupped her shaven mound, Kirk was the one who moaned this time. Lifting his mouth from hers, he met her gaze.

"I need to see your pretty pussy, lovely lady. I need to see the sweet plump lips I've touched. Do you feel your wetness on my fingers?"

Vicky felt Kirk's fingers stroking over her feminine flesh, dipping between them to gather her arousal fluids. Oh yes, she felt her pussy lips slick and slippery-wet as his hand moved about. With a start of surprise, she realized that her thighs had parted to allow him easier access.

"Please don't cover your breasts, Vicky. I know...lift your arms up above your head."

She obeyed him, stunned that she had unconsciously concealed her body. A moment later she felt his hand shift, and the fingers inside her began probing more thoroughly. Considering that this whole night was turning into an unbelievable sexual odyssey, Vicky was still taken unawares as Kirk's fingers found that *spot*. His thumb was working magic on her clit. Fireworks started going off inside her body. Dimly she felt Kirk remove his fingers to allow his cock to enter her. She lifted her thighs to assist him. One thrust and he was inside her.

"Oh God! Kirk!"

Vicky's eyes shot up to meet his looking down at her. She felt full and her muscles were contracting and squeezing tightly around his cock. Slowly he began moving in and out of her spasming cunt. Each time he embedded his hard rod, she could feel her breasts bouncing up and down, before slowly shaking side to side.

As his gaze dropped to her jiggling bosoms, Vicky felt his excitement increase. His thrusts sped up. She tried to squeeze her muscles tight and hold him inside. When he groaned, she knew she was having some success. She wanted him to feel as aroused as she did.

"Vicky! Good God, woman!"

Kirk kissed her lips, hard. As his head moved away, he met her gaze. With each thrust into her body, he held her eyes and neither looked away. Vicky had never felt so intimate before. It felt like Kirk was seeing her soul, and it was totally bare and exposed. She couldn't turn away, though. His hold upon her mind seemed to be just as strong as his possession of her body.

Then Kirk slid one hand down between their bodies. Without error, one finger found her clit. His touch moved and enticed. Vicky had to close her eyes as she felt the heat and tension rising inside her once again. She didn't think it was possible, but a moment later another climax broke over her. Her brain shut down and her body took over as spasms and contractions sent fireworks along her nervous system. Dimly she felt Kirk resume thrusting in and out of her tight flesh until his own orgasm crashed through him.

From somewhere she'd thought was dead inside her came the idea of happily-ever-after with this man. Behind her closed eyelids she saw flashes of hearts and flowers. Was she too old to believe in such things? She didn't want to be foolish and read more into this than it was; yet she couldn't shake her wish for something more. Then from the depth of her core, her innermost soul, came the unbidden desire that he was filling her body with his essence right now instead of the damned condom!

Chapter Six

The following day Kirk was tired and pissed, not to mention distracted. They never got the chance to call in sick. At some point last night they had switched positions on the bed. When the phone rang early, Vicky had spontaneously picked up the phone.

"Hello!"

"Vicky! Darling, is that you?"

Kirk was fully awake and could hear Val's voice coming in a surprised shriek through the receiver. He sat up slowly, turning to look at Vicky. She sat up quickly and was naked to her waist. A gentleman would wait, he discussed in his head. But then he grinned and moved in on her distracted person. As he cupped one breast, her surprise became audible.

"Eek!"

With the phone held an inch or so from her ear, Kirk easily heard Val's reply.

"Oh dear, Vicky! I must have dialed your number by accident. Hang up and go back to sleep. I'll call Kirk's number. Bye-bye, sweetheart, we'll talk later!"

In less than ten seconds, his extension rang again. Reluctantly, he reached across Vicky and answered. Before he could react to Val's light-hearted "good morning," Vicky slid out of bed and was running back to her bedroom. When he knocked on her door thirty minutes later, showered, shaved and ready to go to work, her reply was muffled.

"I'll take a cab! I'm not ready."

So in his mind, Kirk felt his foul mood was justified. Instead of savoring the sweet and sensual awakening that he'd been dreaming about only seconds earlier, they had been rudely awakened by her mother. He was grateful that Valentina had assumed she'd made a mistake, but he wasn't happy at Vicky's avoidance of him since then. Now he was using a pitiful excuse to come to the workroom to see her while still under the guise of business.

After asking directions of two people in Valentina's cutting room, he made his way to the model's fitting area. Walking around the opening for the semi-private area, he stopped dead in his tracks. The scene in front of him was probably the last thing he had been expecting. He'd seen any number of models in here since he'd agreed to manage Valentina's expansion plans. And of course they had often been in various stages of undress. Usually he ignored them when his mind was on straightening out accounting errors, but this was Vicky. He'd never had to experience seeing a woman he was involved with—

Good God! Sirens were going in his head. Was he *involved* with his stepsister? Shaking his head, he promptly decided that referring to Vicky as his stepsister was not a good idea any more. So, if he was involved with her, did that automatically mean that they were in a relationship? They weren't having an affair because only married people had affairs these days. Right?

Standing in front of the mirror was Vicky. What she wasn't wearing was enough clothes to cover her body. Instead, she was dressed in the sexiest white concoction of lingerie he'd ever seen. Seeing her from the rear and the front simultaneously was rather disconcerting, but definitely arousing.

Sexy white heels and silky lace-top stockings were held in place by lacy white garters and topped by white satin tap panties. Her nicely rounded ass looked almost too tempting to be ignored. Next there was a white lace Merry Widow cinching her waist in tightly. God! He remembered the days when he would have just appreciated the sexy garments without even knowing their names.

In the reflection he saw that the corset was pushing her breasts up in the most amazing display he'd witnessed since…hell! He couldn't remember the last time he'd been so aroused by a nearly naked woman—not counting last night, of course. Then he noticed that she was barely wearing a bra at all and with one misstep, he'd be able to see her nipples…and so could anyone else.

"You look beautiful, Vicky! God! More than that, babe, you look drop-dead sexy. You make me want to be the groom that peels off a beautiful bridal gown and finds something even better beneath it."

It took Kirk a few seconds to realize that while he might have said similar words in his head, it was not his voice that had just spoken. As he stared at Vicky, Nick Ingles moved into his field of vision. Kirk noticed immediately that the other man was not speaking as a designer.

"Don't exaggerate, Nick. It doesn't suit you." Kirk heard Vicky speaking to the other man, but there was something in her tone as she addressed the handsome designer that made him feel a little reassured.

"If you'd worn things like this when we were engaged—"

"Hush, you two!" Valentina walked all the way around her daughter. "I think we need the veil, darling!"

Kirk watched as Valentina turned away to sift through a pile of tulle. He was still reeling hearing that Nick Ingles had been engaged to Vicky...*his* Vicky! Then from the corner of his eye he saw Nick reach out and cup Vicky's right ass cheek. In that second, Kirk thought the top of his head would blow clean off, he was so angry. But before he could take the necessary step forward, Vicky batted his hand away.

Nick was undaunted, as evidenced by his reply. "Why don't we surprise everyone, babe, and have a minister join us onstage right after you show the wedding dress and we'll get married? That will certainly give us all the press we need to launch these lines. I still think you are the best thing since...uhm—"

"What, Nick? White bread?" Vicky stepped away from the hand that seemed hell-bent on caressing her one way or another.

"Come on, Vicky honey. I'll even get in line with the Valentine's Day crap. I'll buy you a fucking Valentine's card every damned day for the next ten years if that is what it takes for you to come back to me."

"What happened to the man I knew as the president of the club for men against National Suck-Up Day? All the hearts, candy and flowers are just women's way of getting more jewelry out of their husbands. Wasn't that the diatribe you used to spout?"

"Here we go!" Valentina chimed in. "This is the perfect veil." She set the long, draping tulle veil on her daughter's head, and then started adjusting and draping the material. "I don't want to hear another word out of either of you. This is going to be a wonderful Valentine's Day this year. And you'd better get used to it, Nick. I'm giving permission to the staff to celebrate for the next two weeks, right up until the afternoon of the fourteenth when we have the show."

"I promise, Mom, I'll be a good girl. Are you sure about this veil, though? Will it go with the wedding dress?" Vicky asked.

"Don't fret, Vicky. The veil is just for this outfit. For the wedding dress, I want your hair swept up. I'll design something else for the finale."

"Sorry to interrupt, Val, but I wanted you to double check a few things." Kirk spoke loudly as he stepped into the fitting area. His eyes immediately went to Vicky and caught the surprised look on her face as she glanced toward him like a scared rabbit. While their eyes locked, he heard Valentina speaking once again.

"Oh shoot! I left my reading glasses on my desk. Nick, be a darling and fetch them for me, please?"

Kirk watched Vicky as she pulled the veil forward and across her, as if the tissue-paper-thin tulle could conceal her body. Unconsciously he took a step toward her.

"Oh dear! Wait here, Kirk. There is something else I need off my desk."

* * * * *

In that moment, Vicky prayed for the earth to just open up and swallow her whole. She couldn't have been more embarrassed. This morning she'd chickened out and cowered in her bedroom until Kirk had left for work. Now he finds her half-dressed anyway, so that ridiculous bit of cowering did no good whatsoever. And she wondered if he had overheard any of her conversation with Nick. Good God, she hoped not!

"I really didn't want to start out the day that way," Kirk murmured a few seconds later, taking another step closer. "I'd planned on waking you with kisses."

With just a few words, Kirk transported her back to the wonderfully sweet feelings she'd experienced in his arms. "Where?"

Kirk grinned and came within a foot of her. "Your mouth. You have the most kissable lips."

"Then?"

"Well, I can think of two places in particular." He held her eyes.

Vicky felt her cheeks heat. She knew precisely where she wanted him to kiss her. Last night she had discovered that Kirk had a real knack for sucking on her nipples. With one hand squeezing and molding her left breast, his mouth busily drew her nipple inside, which allowed his tongue to dance and tease all around the tender bud. Even now, just thinking about it, there was enough passionate fire to make her toes curl! Never before had she felt such passion, or release. It had been hot, sexy and undeniable. And when he had looked into her eyes, she was sure he pulled—or even yanked—her soul from her body. Still, he did not ravage it. Instead, he cradled it tenderly while he set off magnificent firework displays inside her.

"Seeing you dressed so skimpily is giving me more ideas." Kirk spoke softly, reaching out and lightly running his index finger from the outer side of her left breast, up and over the mound, dipping down in the center and then repeating his action on the other.

Vicky started to move toward his lingering hand. The heat was nearly a tangible thing and she wanted to feel it even more!

"Sorry for taking so long, Kirk."

Vicky and Kirk jumped apart at the sound of her mother's voice. Vicky spun away and started removing the long veil. Out of the corner of her eye, she watched as her mother gave the papers back to Kirk. Twice now Valentina had nearly caught the two of them. The last thing Vicky wanted to do was cause a rift in her mother's new marriage. If anyone ever deserved happiness, it was Valentina Vale.

"Vicky dear, I'll be back in a few minutes. I need to run upstairs with Kirk."

Vicky watched as her mother and her new lover and stepbrother left. She didn't think her mother and closest friend, or her new stepfather, would take kindly to the idea of the stepsiblings screwing one another! That probably was not what they had in mind for family reunions and future get-togethers.

* * * * *

"Val, darling, why do keep looking at your watch?" Mark took his reading glasses off and lowered the book he'd been reading. Ever since they had returned from meeting Vicky and Kirk for dinner again, Valentina had continually checked the time approximately every five or ten minutes.

"I'm just waiting for the right time."

"The right time for what? To make love again? I'm not as young as I used to be, my love."

Valentina leaned the short distance across the bed and kissed her husband. "Stop right there, stud. You have more energy than I do most days. I've been mentally figuring the time it would take them to get to the apartment."

"Who?" Mark didn't like feeling confused, but sometimes with Valentina it was inevitable.

Valentina winked at him, and then picked up her cellular phone. Quickly she dialed a number. Mark watched as she counted the rings with her fingers. One. Two. Three.

"Vicky! Is that you, Vicky?"

Watching his wife's face, she didn't look in the least bit surprised to be talking to her daughter, despite the tone of her voice. He didn't say anything, though, as Valentina began speaking again.

"Oh dear. I am so sorry, sweetheart, but I meant to dial Kirk's extension. I don't know where my mind is these days. I really must tell him something tonight, since I won't be in tomorrow morning until ten."

Valentina stopped speaking as a huge grin slowly spread across her face. Mark leaned forward to ask her a question, but she pressed her index finger against his lips for a second to request him to keep silent.

"Well, good night, Vicky. I'll call Kirk now. I just love having you back home, darling. I've truly missed having you nearby. I love you, too. Night-night."

Valentina disconnected the call. "What the devil do you have to talk to Kirk about that can't wait until tomorrow?"

"One more minute, my love. I beg your patience only one more minute." Valentina had already dialed the other number. This time she counted the rings and got to six.

Mark was sure he heard the call connect and his son say hello, but after a few seconds his wife shut her phone off. She set her phone on the bedside table. When Valentina turned toward him again she looked so pleased with herself that he thought she just might pop.

"What was that all about? I'm sure I heard Kirk's voice answer. Why didn't you reply?" Mark asked his wife curiously.

Valentina took her husband's book and his glasses, setting them on her bedside stand. "Turn the light out, darling, and let's go to sleep." She was snuggling up against him and making him think about other fun things they might do. He flipped the light out, but he still wanted an answer. "I still want to know what those phone calls were about. Like this morning, mixing up the numbers. That's not like you at all, Val. You have all the numbers programmed into the phone."

"I know, Mark, my love. I didn't dial the wrong numbers tonight or this morning. This morning I was just playing a hunch, and tonight I confirmed it." Val rested her head on her husband's shoulder.

"Wait a second. This morning you called Kirk's number, knowing that you dialed the right number. Then when it was answered, you pretended you got the wrong number. Immediately you dialed the same number again—"

"Yes, darling. My daughter was in your son's room at the crack of dawn this morning, and after several rings she answered it with a very sleepy voice. So tonight, I called

Vicky, pretending I wanted Kirk. I could hear some muffled conversation. I dialed quickly and on the sixth ring a very out-of-breath Kirk answered the phone in his bedroom."

Mark shook his head. "Kirk could have been down the hall, in the kitchen or even out in the living room—"

"Or he could have been in my daughter's bedroom."

"Don't be silly, Valentina."

"Perhaps they were playing Parcheesi. I'm sure that is what Vicky was doing in Kirk's bedroom at six this morning."

"My son is a gentleman, Valentina." Mark felt that he had to protest.

"Precisely. He has the same wonderful manners as his father. Now let me think…how long was it after we initially met before the first time that we did it?"

"It's not the same thing, Val. We weren't related!"

Valentina kissed her husband's chin. "And we were in a foreign country. I'm sure that contributed a lot."

Mark chuckled. He'd never before felt such a rush of passion and desire for a woman that he felt like he had been drowning in it all from the first moment he saw Valentina. His first wife, Karen, Kirk's mother, had been his childhood sweetheart. They'd been friends who over time loved one another. He'd been devoted to her until her death. Thinking back on it, he recalled standing that fateful day in the middle of San Marco Square. He'd heard a woman remark behind him, "That Bell Tower looks just like the one in Walt Disney World."

Recognizing the accent, he turned to face a beautiful woman, several years younger than he. The woman was Valentina and she had continued to grin following her traitorous remark. A few seconds later he replied, "You think Italy stole the idea from Walt?"

She had shaken her head and then told him of the many trips she'd made with her daughter to visit the fantasy world. Like many Americans who travel to foreign countries, they seemed to bond. Mark had jokingly told her that perhaps she and her daughter would volunteer to be guides for he and his son. That had been until they discovered how old their children were.

It was Valentina's voice that drew his thoughts back to the present time and place. "Perhaps they were together to discuss…the fashion show."

Mark chuckled as he shook his head, getting back to the business at hand. "Why are you so sure that they—" Mark choked over the words.

"Trust me, Mark. I'm pretty darn sure now. I had a few other clues as well."

"Such as?"

"Well, in the fitting room today, Nick was joking with Vicky about her marrying him on the stage as a highlight for the show. From where I was standing, I could see Kirk's reflection in the mirror. But most importantly I saw how angry he got as Nick persisted in his teasing. Then I managed to leave the two of them alone. I snuck back and watched them for a few seconds. Let's just say that your son was touching my daughter in a very *un-brotherly* way. Most importantly, Vicky wasn't pushing him away. If I'd waited any longer to interrupt, we all would have been very embarrassed."

"I guess we'll have to confront them," Mark suggested without any conviction.

"Not yet, honey. I have high hopes for something really developing between them. From the moment I met Kirk, I just had a feeling he'd be the right man for my stubborn and still-disillusioned daughter. They just need some time, and a few more pushes."

"Val."

"Just a few, Mark, I promise. And didn't you tell me that you hoped Kirk could meet a lovely woman and settle down, just like his father?"

Mark nodded, watching his wife's lovely face, lit only by the dim nightlight as she turned her head so she could look at him. "And if I remember correctly, you must have mentioned at least once that you wished Vicky would meet a nice guy."

Valentina nodded her head with fervor. "I'm a woman who makes dresses so other women can have the wedding of their dreams. Surely I'm entitled to wish that my daughter find someone as wonderful as I did."

Mark turned his wife into his arms and kissed her thoroughly. She was right. Their kids were going to do what they wanted to do, regardless of what they thought. Might as well mind their business and just go with the flow. Of course, considering his wife, it could turn into white water rapids.

Chapter Seven

Vicky found Kirk sitting on the side of his bed, naked and staring at the phone. She wasn't sure, but she thought it had been almost ten minutes since they'd heard his phone start ringing. Since they had still been sharing her bed, Kirk jumped up and jogged down the hallway to his room.

"What's wrong?" she asked, pushing her hair back off her face. When her mother called, they had been kissing and laughing, discussing the fun things Kirk could show her in his shower. Now she wore the sheet from her bed, toga style.

"Nothing. I was waiting for Val to call."

Vicky walked over and sat beside him. "We heard the phone ring."

"Yeah, but when I answered it, whoever it was hung up without saying a word. I figured Val must have gotten a busy signal and would be calling back shortly."

"If she hasn't called back by now, I doubt she will." Vicky reached over and rested her hand on Kirk's thigh. "What about that shower you were telling me about?"

Kirk grinned, took her hand and walked with her into the bathroom. Vicky stared around her in surprise.

"You redecorated, huh?" she finally whispered softly.

"Guilty, I'm afraid. Your mother said it was fine and I like my creature comforts."

Vicky walked toward the large shower enclosure. Opening the door, she peered in and saw the multiple openings in the beautifully tiled walls for water to spray out toward the bather. There was a large seat in the farthest corner.

"I didn't know they made things like this." As she started to close the door, she felt the tugging on the sheet. Since she was wrapped in it, slowly she began to twirl and release her temporary toga. There was no missing the big grin on Kirk's face as he kept pulling and unraveling.

Kirk tossed the sheet behind him a few moments later and pulled Vicky into his arms. He hugged her so tight it was hard to breathe for a second or two. She wasn't sure, but thought he whispered in her ear.

"And I didn't know there was a woman like you."

Then he was releasing her and opening the door to the shower. Twisting the knobs, it took a short time to adjust the temperature. Vicky spent the time looking at Kirk. She was still surprised that he was attracted to her.

He took a step into the shower and she followed him. There wasn't time to catch her breath as she felt the water coming at her from the different heights and directions. Lifting her hands, she slicked her wet hair back from her face. Blinking her eyes to clear her lashes of the water droplets, she saw that Kirk was watching her very intently.

"Is something wrong?" she asked him quietly.

"Nuttin' honey," he jested with her while his hands lifted to cup her breasts. "I just can't resist temptation."

"I thought we came in here to shower." Vicky fought to keep the grin off her face, but failed.

"I'm going to show you several fun ways to accomplish this usually boring task." Kirk turned away to squirt some liquid soap in one palm. Slowly he rubbed his hands together, producing some thick lather. Holding them up, palms facing Vicky, he let his eyes drift down the length of her body and then back up. Finally he spoke, his voice sounding quite serious. "Now, the vital question is where to begin?"

Vicky acted on impulse and answered the question. She stepped forward, grabbed his wrists and pressed her breasts into his palms. "No more questions. Just show me."

Kirk didn't wait. With his hands caressing under the pretense of cleansing, his mouth lowered to hers. The kiss was wet and sensual as the water pelted down and all around them. Vicky lifted her hands to catch some of the dripping suds. Without giving a hint of her intentions, she lowered her hands. Moving her head back, she watched Kirk's face as her one hand curled around his cock. The shocked pleasure on his face was unmistakable, as was the low groan that came from his throat when she started stroking her hand up and down his hardening cock.

Kirk's hands fell away from her breasts. He grabbed the extended shower handle and rinsed the lather from her body. Hoarsely he told her, "Let's get out of here, honey."

Vicky shook her head and took the nozzle from his hand. "You sit down first," she told him while she pushed him gently toward the built-in seat. Once he was seated, Vicky gave herself a quick *you-can-do-this* speech. Just breathe deeply and go!

She replaced the showerhead and filled her hand with some of his shampoo. Lifting both hands she began soaping up her hair. Kirk's eyes dropped almost immediately to her breasts. Purposely she added some extra jiggle a few times before she rinsed out the lather. Squirting some liquid into one palm, she then smeared it around between them both. Stopping once they were covered with soapy lather, she put her hands over her breasts, but didn't touch them. She waited until Kirk looked up at her.

"Oops! I almost forgot that you already took care of me there." Quickly she put one hand under each arm, covering her breasts while she washed her armpits. Once Kirk started looking a little frustrated, she moved her hands and ran them down to make circles lower and lower on her stomach. His eyes followed the movements all the way to where she stopped with one hand resting on her shaven mound. Vicky glanced down and saw that his cock was hard. It made her feel attractive that she could visually pleasure him this way.

"Come over here, sweetheart, and let me wash the rest for you," Kirk told her softly.

Vicky shook her head and slid her hand farther back. This was the first time she'd ever done anything like this before. Sure, she'd masturbated before, but never in front of someone, a lover. Her fingers slipped over her pussy lips and she felt her juices coating them, showing how effective she was so far. As she pressed against the hood of her clitoris, she groaned. Her other hand went out to rest on the nearest shower wall. Half her mind was caught up in the pleasure rising in her body. The other part was wondering how she could further arouse Kirk.

Then it dawned on her. In order to more easily reach and stimulate her clit, all she needed to do was to bend forward at the waist. Wiggling her finger, she slipped it onto her clit. The first reaction shook her body and she felt her breasts swaying in response. Speeding up the teasing, her hips were flexing forward, demanding more.

Suddenly Kirk moved and pulled her forward while he grabbed the shower nozzle. "Lift your foot here and lean into me."

Tense and needing release, Vicky did as directed, resting one foot on the built-in seat. But she wasn't prepared for the feeling that happened next. Kirk's fingers caressed and stroked her pussy lips, but soon spread her flesh to reveal her clit. That's when the water began its torturous seduction.

She screamed as her climax shook through her body. It was powerful, and she nearly fell under its force. Kirk's arms caught her and held her tenderly as the last quiver shook her body. As she became aware of Kirk's hand caressing over her wet hair, she buried her face in his shoulder.

"That didn't go the way I had planned," she confided weakly.

"Oh. Well I'll be happy to try again. Perhaps if I spend more time on your pussy, that might do the trick. I think a pretty pussy like this sometimes requires the extra attention." His hand cupped her mound, sliding sideways, back and forth. "I'll volunteer for grooming needs. Just thinking about shaving you—"

Vicky shook her head. "That's not what I meant, Kirk. I wanted to pleasure you."

"Oh, really," Kirk answered. Even though she couldn't see his face, she heard the humor and interest in his voice. God, she told herself silently, if this man wasn't making love to her, he was making her smile! How was a woman to resist?

"Just what had you planned to do?" Kirk prodded her.

Vicky didn't answer right away. Just because she had climaxed first didn't mean that she couldn't continue. Her body relaxed and she slid from his arms. On her knees, between his legs, she wasted no time in grasping his rod with her hand. She stroked him a few times before she spoke.

"I wanted to touch your body, like this." Holding his cock, she used her other hand to cup his balls. His involuntary body jerk made her smile. She wanted him to enjoy this. Slowly she slid one hand around his sac, and then she lowered her head. Without pause, she took him in her mouth. Squeezing him firmly, she matched her bobbing head to the strokes of her hands. As she tugged gently and stretched the skin of his sac, Kirk groaned, which told her he enjoyed that move.

She pressed her thighs together, surprised at how aroused she was becoming. It had never happened before. She glanced up at Kirk, who was leaning his head back against the tile. His hands moved so fast she didn't see them as he grabbed her arms, pulling her up. A moment or so later, she was straddling him and his cock slid inside her. Everything faded away except the overwhelming sensation of just feeling his hardness inside her again.

"Oh, God! Kirk!" she cried out as her body closed around him, squeezing down tightly.

His hands helped her move up and down. She flexed her hips back and forth, switching to side-to-side movements. Different moves stimulated her in exciting ways. Once again she'd wanted to pleasure him, but she was the one reaping the reward. Rolling her hips and flexing them at different speeds and angles provided the extra component needed, which when combined with the thrusting cock inside her, brought them both speedily to the edge of the climactic precipice. As if from a distance, she heard Kirk speaking.

"Honey…God! Vicky, sweetheart, we need to stop. I have to pull out."

Vicky acted spontaneously. She couldn't let him go. What she needed was to feel him fill her with his come. It was earthy and basic. It was risky in some ways, but she didn't question the health issues. Kirk would have told her…he was that kind of man. And the chance of pregnancy was unlikely at this time of the month. Holding onto him with her arms, she focused on squeezing her cunt muscles. She milked his cock. That's when she orgasmed and bit the side of his neck.

Kirk's groan was low and primitive. He could force Vicky off him, but he didn't want to. Right then he wanted to fill her sweet body with his come, his sperm. The idea of being permanently locked with Vicky was not making him crazy like it had with any other woman. This felt right. As she bit his neck, he lost control. His climax slammed throughout his body. With quick, short thrusts he shot hot sperm into her cunt. He held her tightly in his arms while their bodies calmed.

Chapter Eight

Kirk had been watching the clock on his desk since his arrival at the office. At breakfast that morning, the topic was the phone call that never came. Pausing between bites of his cereal, he had broached the subject.

"As soon as I see Val this morning I'll ask why she didn't call last night."

Vicky shook her head vigorously. "You can't do that." She took a bite of his cereal.

"Why not? It must have been important for her to call in the first place."

"I've been thinking about the phone calls, you know," Vicky told him seriously while she reached over and stole a piece of the cut-up apple Kirk was also having for breakfast.

Kirk shook his head as he took a bite of the cereal. Vicky reached across and wiped a tiny drop of milk from the corner of his mouth. Since she was still sitting on his lap, it had been quite easy to do. As he chewed he pressed a damp kiss to her neck. After he swallowed, he questioned her.

"When have I given you time to think?"

Vicky had appeared to ponder his words seriously, and then she smiled at him. "I was on the toilet—" Abruptly she stopped as Kirk began tickling her. It hadn't taken him long to discover where her sensitive and vulnerable spots were. "Stop! Stop! Mercy!"

Kirk lifted his hand and turned her face toward his. As their eyes met, he spoke softly. "Always." And then he kissed her.

Once they finally parted, both were flushed and breathing hard. Vicky squirmed off Kirk's lap. She fanned her face as she sat on the chair beside his. Lifting one hand, she grabbed a section of the newspaper, using it to fan her heated face.

"Whew! We have to stop this or you won't make it to work before my mom does." Vicky said with a loud sigh.

"Regretfully, I'll listen to your voice of reason. Now why can't I ask Val about not calling me last night?" He took another bite of the cereal.

"It's not like my mother to mix up phone numbers."

"Everybody makes mistakes like that, hon." He was still leaning toward his idea about asking Val. It seemed like the forward and honest way to do it. For what was most likely the thousandth time, Kirk wished he could have met Vicky at a less busy time for the business. He was torn between sneaking away to spend time with her and making sure he was on-site for any emergencies.

"I know. But if you ask her why she didn't call last night, then she will know that I told you she was going to call." Vicky picked up his glass of juice and took a long drink.

Kirk lifted his coffee cup toward her. "Care for some coffee?"

Vicky shook her head. "No thanks." She picked up two pieces of the apple as she added, "I'm not all that hungry this morning."

"Right. Now getting back to the topic at hand. Yes, your mother would know that you had told me that is exactly what you did...uhm do."

Vicky leaned toward him. "But at that time of night, the call came to my bedroom line, so if I told you then you would either have been in my room, or I would have gotten up and gone to your bedroom to tell you."

Kirk shrugged. "True on the first, but it is possible you would do the second."

"Remember how quickly the phone rang in your room? That is how long it would have taken her to redial."

"That was a wrong number." Kirk paused to take a piece of the apple, chewing it slowly while he thought. "Which makes me wonder why she didn't call me, like she told you she was going to do."

"Beats me, honey." Vicky shook her head, tousling her shoulder-length hair. She wiggled the fingers of one hand. "Pass me another bite of apple, please."

Nearly three hours after their shared meal, Kirk smiled as he sat at his desk. They hadn't really solved the little mystery, but hearing Vicky call him "honey," which was the first time she'd used any kind of endearment, had taken his mind off that problem. At the front door, kissing her goodbye, he'd suggested the plausible excuse. His father had distracted Valentina and the phone call was forgotten. That's what he would have done, he'd rationalized as he reluctantly left for the office.

Glancing at the clock, he was grateful to see it was half past ten. Valentina should be in her new office by now. He would go down and see if she brought the subject up.

* * * * *

Vicky was already frustrated and she'd only been here for ten minutes. After Kirk left, she'd been puttering around his kitchen when the phone rang. Her mother insisted she needed to come in at ten to start fittings. What she didn't like was the fact that her mother had handed her over to Nick to begin the preliminaries for the wedding dress.

"Come on, Vicky."

"I am not taking my clothes off in front of you. Besides you always have your assistant take the models' measurements!" She batted away Nick's hands, which kept trying to unbutton or pull off some article of her clothing.

"It's not like I haven't seen it all before," Nick joked as he finally got Vicky's sweater off.

"Nick! You are not acting like a gentleman."

"I can be as much of a gentleman as you require, my sweet. I'll even shower you with roses and candy for every anniversary. More presents than you could open in one day on birthdays and a handmade card on Valentine's Day."

Vicky stared in disbelief at the handsome blond man. "What happened to the man who proclaimed Valentine's Day was the invention of women to make men feel guilty? National Suck-up Day? Remember saying those things, Nick? I seem to recall you telling me, and anyone else who would listen, that all this sentimentality was just crap."

Vicky looked at Nick. She couldn't make sense of this total change in his behavior. Sure, they had been engaged for a brief period, but it had only taken two Valentine's Days to pass before she knew that she couldn't live like that the rest of her life. Once she'd had that revelation, it was easier to admit that she wasn't really in love with Nick after all. Maybe it was fear that had driven her to accept the offer to go out to dinner with him in the first place. Everyone she'd known from high school and college was either married or divorced, and some remarried. Always hanging over her head was the fact that since she was *the* Valentina Vale's daughter she would therefore have the most magnificent wedding dress possible.

Frustrated with Nick and her thoughts, she reached out and grabbed the tape measure from his hands. "I'll take my own measurements."

"Now you're just being childish and ridiculous, Vicky," Nick argued, reaching for the tape.

"Anything I can help with?"

Vicky spun around. Yes, that was Kirk's voice she had just heard. Just seeing how sexy he looked with his suit jacket off, tie askew and top shirt button undone, she was struck anew by the depth of the feelings inside her for a man she hardly knew. The fact that his shirtsleeves were rolled up slightly, revealing his muscular forearms, made her toes curl upward. The reactions her body was having—increased heart rate, rapid breathing, butterflies in her stomach and the sudden fullness and warmth in her pussy—was something she was rapidly coming to associate with just being near Kirk.

Nick spoke up, which surprised Vicky. "No thanks. I'm just getting some measurements on Vicky for the show."

Kirk lifted one eyebrow as he looked at Vicky. She couldn't read his face, but decided to go with honesty. "I'm not stripping down so you can take a few lousy measurements. I'll do it myself, Nick."

"It doesn't work like that, Vicky, and you know it." Her former fiancé pushed his blond hair back off his forehead. She noticed that he'd started wearing it longer so it fell forward. He probably thought it made him look sexy. It did not, in her opinion.

"What's your objection, Vicky?" Kirk's voice sounded steady and not upset. She had rather thought he might be upset finding her alone with her former fiancé. It piqued her that he seemed so nonchalant.

Vicky inhaled deeply. "I don't think Nick should be doing this."

"I'm a little surprised too, sweetheart, but I do what your mother tells me. So take off your shirt and jeans and we'll get started." Nick reached for the tape again.

Vicky saw Kirk's expression change. "I don't think it's appropriate as my ex-fiancé that you do this," she told Nick quickly, tilting her chin into the air. Then she saw Kirk's facial features alter quickly. Obviously he had not known about the fact that Nick was her former fiancé. She saw him tighten his jaw and then he smiled again.

"I'll take the measurements and you can write them down, Ingles. That way they get done and no one suffers."

Vicky turned away to hide the small smile that suddenly curved her lips. She waited for Nick to reply before she offered her two cents to the mix. It only took a few seconds.

"The measurements should be taken without clothes on," Nick protested, all the while he kept shaking his head.

Vicky opened her mouth to voice her objections once again. Before she could get the first word out, Kirk grabbed her elbow and pulled her behind the only dressing screen in the area.

"I'll call the measurements out to you, Ingles. If you don't hear me, I'll be happy to re-measure an area."

Behind the screen, Vicky looked up at Kirk. Opening her mouth again, she still didn't get a chance to speak. Kirk kissed her quickly and then pressed his finger to her lips.

"I couldn't resist and I wasn't letting Ingles touch you," he whispered to her quickly, leaning in close so she could hear him clearly.

Vicky smiled and handed the tape measure to Kirk. "Just so you know that this is something a woman never wants a man to know." Pulling her shirt off, she undid her jeans and let them slide to the floor. Today she'd worn a utilitarian white bra and full panties. She knew it wasn't sexy, but then she wasn't planning on this happening when she'd gotten dressed after Kirk had left that morning.

Kirk leaned down to whisper close to her ear. "Every single inch is beautiful and sexy, and makes me hornier and harder than I've ever been in my life." He straightened back up and called out clearly. "What should I measure first, Nick? It's a good thing we're siblings, eh, sis!"

The punch Vicky gave his stomach only made him grin. Then he playfully put the tape around her right breast.

"Is this the right way, sis?"

"Stop that!" Vicky took the tape and placed it in the right position, holding the overlapping ends between her breasts. She tapped the marking with her fingernail. "That is the number, right there."

"Party pooper," Kirk told her softly before he raised his voice and called out the measurement to Nick.

The rest of the measurements were accomplished quickly, as long as she didn't count the time Kirk slipped his hands under the tape to cup her ass cheeks. His mouth kissed its way along her shoulder before he released her and read the correct number. After Kirk measured her upper arm, neck to waist and waist to floor lengths, Nick told them the last one he needed.

"You can do this one by yourself, Vicky."

Kirk shrugged, but asked quickly, "What is it?"

"Upper thigh."

Before she could take the tape, Kirk dropped to one knee. With care he placed the paper tape around her thigh. He glanced up, lifting one eyebrow.

"That's good enough," Vicky murmured. The feel of Kirk's hands, the lightest of touches from his fingertips, were arousing her. She had hoped Nick would skip this one measurement. Just seeing Kirk had started the reactions inside her. Now the crotch of her panties was damp from her arousal. All he would have to do was raise his hand—

Kirk's fingers ran the length of her crotch, pausing a moment before he called out the last number. At the same time he shouted it, his hand turned and cupped her pussy. Vicky felt him tug on the elastic and then his flesh was on hers. Gasping, she braced her hands on his shoulders. Despite the amazing sweetness of his caress, she felt the need to protest, at least a little.

"We shouldn't—"

"I think we should," he whispered as he slid two fingers between her wet, swollen lips. He wiggled them around inside of her, finally easing them forward and lightly touching her clit.

"Oh!" Vicky bit her lip as she tried to prevent her cries from escaping while Kirk's clever fingers tempted her with glimpses of passionate release. A few more seconds and she would not be able to keep from crying out.

"There you are, Nicholas. I'm looking for Vicky. Have you seen her?"

Vicky froze at the sound of her mother's voice.

"Ouch!"

Glancing down, she realized that she had clenched her fingers in Kirk's hair and was pulling. Quickly she released her hands. At the same time she felt his fingers leave her flesh and then pull her panties back into place. As he stood, she saw his wet fingers.

"Wipe them on my shirt," she whispered to him frantically, bending down to pull her jeans on. While she fastened them, she saw Kirk unbutton his shirt and then rub his fingers on his chest. He must have noticed her confused look because a second later he winked at and whispered, "This way I'll have the scent of you with me all day."

Quickly he kissed her and then walked back around the screen that had concealed them. "Good morning, Valentina. At breakfast this morning, Vicky said you called me last night. What did you need to discuss?"

Vicky plopped down on the nearby chair. She tuned out the voices beyond the screen barrier. In her head she kept hearing Kirk's words.

This way I'll have the scent of you with me all day.

Never had she had any man say such a sensual thing to her before. Nick had made one or two comments after the only time they engaged in oral sex. He was all in favor of her repeating her activities, but he had lots of reasons and comments on why he should not perform oral sex on her. Now Kirk wanted to remember her womanly scent, the odor of her passion, all day. He was choosing her, not the perfumed and artificial woman who got presented to the rest of the world.

She wrapped her arms across her stomach. The feeling inside was making her feel nauseated and light-headed. What was going on? This wasn't how she'd felt with Nick or any other guy she'd dated or been interested in. Living away from here, she'd acknowledged that it wasn't love she'd felt for Nick. It had been shared interests and propinquity, which she had learned from a therapist she saw a few times. Two people who spend a lot of time together can often confuse their feelings for love.

What she felt right now was raw and painful. It was joyful and ecstatic as well. Thinking about going back home was tearing her up inside. She knew she'd miss her mother, but it was the thought of leaving Kirk that was making her crazy. No, it was more than that. Sitting alone, she imagined herself back in her apartment and going about her daily life. Suddenly it was so empty and alone that she started to cry. She tuned out the voices a few feet away, trying to be quiet and unheard.

Chapter Nine

Kirk smiled at Valentina while he waited for her to answer. Asking about the previous night's phone call this way hopefully wouldn't arouse her curiosity. Or at least he hoped so. He'd be happy to have everything out in the open, but he was pretty sure that Vicky wasn't ready yet. Protecting her heart and conceding to her wishes were paramount. He had been stunned last night as he sat waiting for Valentina to call him. Could he be in love with his stepsister?

At first he'd acknowledged the powerful attraction he felt for her. Discovering she was experiencing the same had brought together dynamite and C-4 plastic explosive! Sex with Vicky was better than he had ever experienced before. She wasn't the typical model-thin woman that he had dated in the past. But from the first moment he'd seen her, the pull to be near her was there. The need to be inside her grew with each passing encounter. Now that he had been deep within her body, feeling her muscles tightly enclosing his cock, he wasn't going to be able to let her return home.

Thinking about that as he sat on the bed, he realized that it was more than the sex. There was the fun they had when they weren't making love. And while they had not had much time together so far, he was beginning to doubt that he would be able to let her leave. If she did go, there was a good chance that he was going to follow her. She'd have to tell him face to face that she didn't want him or love him.

That was when it hit him. He loved her. Sure, most people would say it could only be lust, but something told him this had all the right ingredients to work. All he had to do was convince Vicky. He had little doubt she was experiencing the lust right now. Given time, he'd prove his love to her.

"You know, Kirk, I've completely forgotten what it was. I blame your father, darling. He can be quite persuasive." Kirk had to shake his head as Val's voice pulled him back to the present and away from his memories.

Kirk cleared his throat as well as his mind, especially after what Valentina had just confided. He guessed it was typical that kids don't really want to hear or think about their parent having sex.

Valentina smiled, patting his cheek as she walked by him. "So Vicky told you last night I'd be calling."

Kirk turned slowly to face Valentina. She was either deliberately forgetting what he'd just told her, or she was trying to trip him up. He remembered Vicky's protests about her mother rarely making mistakes. Shaking his head negatively, he replied.

"Not last night, Val. She was already in bed and when she told me this morning, I realized that I had been sound asleep at the time of the call." Kirk saw Valentina smile at him as she stepped closer to the screen.

"You boys run along. I've got some things to discuss with my daughter. We'll catch up later, Nick. Vicky can try on some of the mock-up designs we have and give us an idea of where to go for the final designs. Ta-ta."

Kirk watched his stepmother disappear around the screen. Feeling frustrated, he turned to leave. Seeing the irritated, perturbed and thwarted look on Ingles' face brightened his spirits immediately, though. He returned to his office with a spring in his step.

* * * * *

Vicky looked up as her mother stepped around the screen. Quickly she tried to rub the tears from her cheeks. Of course she knew she looked suspicious. She was sitting behind a screen, partially dressed and crying. This was not the look of a successful, modern woman.

"Hi, Mom."

"Who makes my baby cry? Tell me his name and I'll have him drawn and quartered."

Vicky stood and let her mother hug her. She planned on thanking her mom and denying anything was wrong, when the dam broke. A second later, more tears were running over her cheeks. A few sniffles and hiccups passed before Vicky could talk.

"It's not that, Mother. I'm fine. It's probably just jet lag. I'll be fine for your big show."

Valentina put her hands on either side of her daughter's face. "I don't give a damn about the show. At this point it could go on without me. All I want is your happiness, my darling daughter. I may be newly married, Victoria, but I will always be your mama."

A second later both women were crying. It took some time, but eventually they left the screened area. Valentina insisted on Vicky joining her for lunch at noon. Vicky agreed and said she'd browse through the store until then to give her mother time to work. Since her mother was watching her leave, she got on the elevator and pushed the "lobby" button. As soon as the door opened, she pushed the number that would take her up to Kirk's office.

As soon as the doors opened, Vicky walked quickly through the hallways until she reached Kirk's. The secretary's desk was empty and she saw that his office door was cracked open slightly. Quickly she walked over, pushing open the door.

"We can't do—"

"Vicky! What a surprise! Look, Dad, it's Vicky!"

Vicky froze as she realized how close she had just come to revealing everything that was going on between Kirk and herself. This morning, while taking their time saying a leisurely goodbye, he had suggested they lock the office door and indulge in a "quickie" in between bites of sandwiches that he'd order in advance.

The next words out of her mouth, if Kirk had not interrupted, would have been "our quickie picnic." She doubted that her new stepfather could easily see through any explanations they might make following a statement like that. It had been lucky that Kirk had been able to cut her off before she'd ruined—

Good Lord! What did she even have to ruin in the first place? What were she and Kirk doing? How could a relationship like this go on, proceed or have any kind of future? Crap! When did she start thinking of the future? She frowned as all these crazy thoughts kept crashing through her brain. No way was she made for dealing with this kind of stress.

"Hello, Vicky! I stopped in to see my son." Mark crossed the room, clasped his hands around her upper arms and lightly kissed her cheek. "And I get the bonus of seeing my lovely new daughter. What more could a man ask for?"

"That's sweet of you to say so, Mr. Magnuson…uhm…Mark."

Mark smiled. "Call me Mark, Vicky. And hopefully one day you'll feel comfortable enough to call me dad."

Vicky blinked quickly to hold back the unexpected start of tears to her eyes. There had never been a "dad" in her life. As she grew up, her mother had dated now and then, but her business had always come second in her life, after Vicky, which rarely left much free time to date. Then when she'd started college, her mother moved her business and expansion to the forefront. That's why Valentina had been in Venice in the first place. She'd gone there to study the style and elegance represented in the architecture and the museums of the beautiful city. Fate had stepped in, though, and now Vicky had a stepfather.

"Don't push it, Vicky. Dad will still love you."

Vicky turned to smile at Kirk, but Mark's next words caught her by surprise, as they supposedly did to her lover, if his expression accurately mirrored his thoughts and emotions.

"That's right, Vicky. Both Kirk and I will love you no matter what you call us."

Kirk love her? Wait, that wasn't even decent grammar. But her brain was rattled by what Mark had just said. Love? No way…right? Vicky jerked her gaze away from Kirk, feeling the heated flush steal across her cheeks. Had she seen the same shock in his eyes, or perhaps it had been denial at his father's words? Maybe she had thought the word in her head, or whispered it in her soul, but hearing it spoken out loud in conjunction with Kirk's name had taken her by surprise.

Pressing her hand to her chest, she tried to slow her breathing. She could feel herself hyperventilating and if she didn't stop it soon, she'd be looking up at her new stepfamily from the floor.

"My spies were correct, I see." Valentina spoke from the doorway to the office. Stepping into the room, she crossed to her husband and kissed his cheek.

"Hi, Mom," Vicky whispered, hoping her mother wouldn't notice that she was breathing too fast. But of course, that was foolish, because her mother had dealt with this too many times in the past to not catch the symptoms.

"Uh oh." Valentina grabbed her daughter's arm and dragged her toward the sofa. "Sit down, Vicky!"

* * * * *

Love! What was his father saying? Kirk saw Vicky staring at him, and she looked as shocked as he did. Who had said anything about love? Well, sure he had been trying the word out in his head a few times, seeing how it felt, and so on. But he hadn't spoken it out loud. He was having the best time of his life with Vicky, but love? Holy shit! Was he ready to be in love?

Then he saw the flush moving up Vicky's neck and across her cheeks. It gave her skin the softest color of pink and it reminded him of a similar heated color. Except that the previous time Vicky had been naked and he had seen the color rising from her breasts. Promptly he had kissed his way from her blushing cheeks down to her taut nipples.

Kirk shook his head to clear it and stop the arousal rising in his body. Suddenly he realized that Valentina was pushing Vicky toward the leather sofa in his office. He frowned as he noted that the flush was gone and now Vicky was almost white. Before he could move a step, though, he saw Valentina shoving Vicky toward the sofa.

"Hey!" he shouted angrily. Why in the world was her mother pushing her around like that? Had he missed something?

Like slow motion he saw Vicky start to crumple like a crushed paper cup. She'd be on the floor if it had not been for Valentina's last second hard push toward the couch. Taking a step forward, he heard his stepmother speak to his father.

"It's too late to put her head between her knees, Mark. Help me get her turned and I'll prop her feet on the cushions or just lift them myself." Valentina quickly saw she couldn't get Vicky's feet very high, so she leaned over the arm of the sofa and held her daughter's feet.

"What's wrong? Let me hold her feet, darling," Mark took Vicky's feet.

"Thank you, sweetheart," Valentina told her husband. She moved to kneel at Vicky's head and fanned her daughter with her hand.

Kirk crossed and watched the interchange. "What's wrong with her?"

Valentina turned and smiled up at him. "She's only passed out. She should be fine in a few minutes. I can't imagine what happened. She hasn't done this since high school."

Kirk had a damned good idea as to what had just happened. His father's unfortunate words must have affected her as much as they had him. The question remained whether she'd thought he was in love with her, or she was caught off guard by her own emotions. God! Could this situation get any more complicated?

"Oh shit!"

Kirk realized that it was Vicky who had spoken. Before he could reply or ask how she was, Valentina was speaking to her daughter.

"It's all right, Vicky. Nothing got broken, on you or other wise."

Vicky laughed. "That's good, anyway. Thanks for holding my feet up, Mark."

"My pleasure, Vicky."

"I'll get up now, Mom."

"No, you will not. I want you to stay here with your feet up. I'll order us some lunch."

"I'd be happy to run out and bring something back for all of us. We could have a picnic," Mark offered quickly.

"That would work, darling."

Kirk saw his father turn to look at him. He had no doubt what his father was about to say.

"Why don't you come with me, son?"

Yup, he was right. Worry for Vicky warred inside him against going with his dad. Leaving for lunch wouldn't allow for either parent to question…anything. Part of his head was telling him everything was going to be fine and to just keep his mouth shut.

"I have a better idea, Mark." Valentina stood and grabbed Kirk's hand. She tugged until he acceded. "You sit on the sofa and hold Vicky's feet."

Less than five minutes later his office door closed, leaving Vicky and him alone. Her shoeless feet rested on a small cushion atop Kirk's lap, which Valentina had placed there right before she'd left with her husband. Looking at her toes, he noticed she had a golden toe ring on her third toe, as well as a gold chain around her ankle. Instead of keeping his hands to himself, he lightly traced his finger along the chain. He stopped when Vicky wiggled her toes. He turned his head to look at her. He wasn't surprised that she was watching him because that was what he'd been struggling not to do ever since Valentina had pushed him onto the sofa.

"What happened to you?" he asked a moment later, shifting on the sofa to see her more easily. Both hands clasped her feet, one in each.

"I hyperventilated and passed out. It doesn't happen often, really. I didn't do it when Nick and I broke up." She stopped quickly and her smile faded.

"When was the last time you actually hit the dirt?"

* * * * *

Vicky heard Kirk's soft voice asking her the question, but she was really focused on the way his thumbs were caressing the soles of her feet. If his intention was to seduce her, he could not have chosen a more inappropriate place to start, considering they were in his office and waiting for their parents to return.

"I passed out at college one time. Uhm…but my mother doesn't know about that one. I can't imagine what caused it today. It was probably just a fluke." Vicky looked around the room, anywhere but at Kirk. She'd never been very good at lying. "I'm probably hungry."

A second later she realized it was stupid to say that. Now she was recalling that she had not eaten much at breakfast. And the way Kirk's hands were caressing their way around her ankles and moving slowly up her calves told her that he was most likely remembering the morning meal as well.

Kirk was going to have cereal, having been dressed for the office already. Vicky had strolled out a few minutes later, her hair wet and trailing down her back. She had made herself some toast and then started digging through the refrigerator for some jelly or marmalade. Finally, she came to the table with four open jars and her one piece of toast. She had ignored his snort of disdain as she placed a small amount of each type on one corner of her toast. Seeing his doubting look, she had smiled.

"I couldn't make up my mind. This way I can sample them all."

Kirk had stood and walked around the table. Without a word, he had pulled Vicky from her chair. Gently he had edged her onto the table. When her robe parted, he had pushed it off her shoulders. He then dipped the spoon into the orange marmalade first. In disbelief, Vicky watched as he had dripped some of the gooey stuff on her right nipple.

"Hey! I just took a shower," she had protested weakly.

Kirk had winked as he promised her, "I'll clean it up."

After that she hadn't protested when he pushed her back onto the table. Soon her left nipple had been encircled with purple jelly. She was so aroused that it was hard to sit still on the table. Kirk had leaned over and his tongue began lapping at her right nipple. With a mix of quick short licks and long, slow pulls he had completely removed all traces of the sugary goop. A moment later, he dropped a spoonful of blackberry jam and filled her belly button. She had giggled as he sampled it with his finger first.

Yet none of this had prepared her for the strawberry preserves he had spread with his finger along her pussy lips. When his tongue had reached her clit, even though there was no more fruit, Kirk had showed her just how sweet a shared breakfast could be. Her cries had echoed around the room as her orgasm crashed through her. Afterwards, she had let him pull her limp body from the table and he had held her on his lap. A few bites of cereal and apple were all she had ended up eating after all, while they discussed her mother's odd phone call the previous night. After a leisurely kiss at the door, she had gone back to bed for a while.

Kirk's voice drew her out of her pleasant recollections. "I was looking forward to our picnic and making love on this sofa. Then every time I glanced over this way I'd remember how it was between the two of us."

Vicky's eyelids drifted shut. His hands were now at the back of her knees, caressing and stroking her gently. It felt incredibly sensual and she was already so tensely aroused that if he slid his hand upward and touched her—

A knock on the door interrupted her thoughts. The door swung open and her mother's former secretary, Denise, looked around the edge. It was obvious she was taken by surprise by the scene she was presented with. Kirk spoke first.

"Hello, Denise. Did you need something?"

Denise smiled, looking from her new boss to Vicky. "Hmm. Feet elevated can only mean one thing."

Vicky laughed. "You've been working here too long."

"Anyway, Nick Ingles just called. He's looking for you." Denise pointed directly at Vicky. "I told him that I hadn't seen you yet. Do you want me to call him back?"

Kirk shook his head negatively. "No. In fact, you can take off and enjoy a long noon break today. Our folks are coming back with lunch."

Denise grinned. "I'll forward the phones to the switchboard then. Thanks."

Vicky smiled. "You should call Dave and see if he's free to join you." She winked at the other woman when she saw her blush. Only after the door had closed behind her, did Kirk begin stroking his fingers along her legs.

"Dave? She has a boyfriend?" Kirk asked a moment later.

"Dave Fernandez, in accounting. They've been dancing around one another for a couple of years, but since Mom got married things have escalated."

"I had no idea. How did you know all this?"

Vicky propped herself up on her elbows. "This is really a small little family, my mother's business. Denise and I, as well as a few other people, exchange emails once in awhile."

"How do you feel now?" Kirk asked softly.

"Much better," Vicky murmured. She pulled one foot away and then the other, feeling the loss of his warm hands instantly. Squirming around on the couch, she came up on her knees. As she leaned toward him, her hands rested upon his shoulders. It felt absolutely necessary to kiss him right now. With his lips pressing against hers, his hands encircled her waist. Slowly Kirk pulled her down, so she was sprawled across his lap. As his hand cupped one breast, Vicky pushed herself more fully into his grasp.

Kirk lowered his hand until he cupped her crotch. "I don't know how I'm going to get through the rest of the day."

Vicky grinned, kissing his lips before she replied. "I was looking forward to our quickie picnic. I do hope my mother doesn't suggest we all have dinner together again."

"We need to come up with a plausible excuse."

Vicky moaned as Kirk's hand stroked over her pussy, resting between her thighs. "Two excuses so they won't suspect anything."

"I'll say I'm meeting a friend for drinks at a sports bar," Kirk suggested. "Any ideas for your excuse?"

Vicky moved her hand to cover his nipple. Feeling its tautness, she began teasing it with her fingertip. "I doubt they'd believe I'm going to a sports bar, so maybe I'll have a headache."

"You could say you still feel a little dizzy," Kirk offered helpfully.

Vicky squirmed as he moved his hand slightly. "Nope. If I do that, mom will either want to drag me off to a doctor or insist on spending the night to make sure I'm okay."

"We'll figure something out…in a minute or two."

Kirk proceeded to show her how sweet he could make love to her with just his hand. Vicky grinned as her zipper slid down. His fingers curved over her mound. Her wetness eased his passage and soon one finger was sliding all over her clit. Each time he found a sensitive place, he would move away from it. Vicky could feel her passion rising. She thrust her hips upward.

"Patience, Vicky." Kirk pulled his hand away and Vicky felt bereft until she saw his hands pushing her shirt up. Her bra was pulled down and it pushed her breasts upward, as an offering. "Good things come to patient girls. Naughty things to wild women."

Ever so lightly, Kirk started to tease and coax her nipples into hard, tight and amazingly long nubs of flesh. Leaning over slightly, he blew air over them. "Now that is a pretty picture. Bad girl on the office couch. Is she about to be ravished by her boss?" He squeezed one breast and then began bouncing it. "Does he have his evil way with her, planting his sperm so high inside her tender and vulnerable cunt that she just might end up in trouble?"

"Oh God!" Vicky groaned, so intensely turned on it shocked her. She gasped loudly. "Naughty sounds like more fun."

Kirk grinned. "Perhaps I'll have to tie you up tonight and show you how misbehavior is treated." Kirk lowered his hand, resuming the maddening rubbing of her clit. Slowly he moved two fingers inside her once again.

Vicky sighed and moved her hips up, increasing the friction to her sensitive flesh. "Ahh."

Kirk increased the speed with which he thrust his fingers in and out of her body. Then he moved his super slick fingers back to her clit. Vicky bit down on her finger as her orgasm shook her body. Over and over she jerked her hips in uncontrollable response.

Slowly she became aware of her surroundings. Kirk's hand was still inside her pants and pressed against her pussy. Kirk was smiling down at her.

"That was beautiful," he told her softly.

"What? Me flopping about like a gasping fish?"

"That is not what I saw. I saw a beautiful woman not afraid of her sensuality and enjoying an orgasm at the hands of her lover. Her belly heaved with the spasms deep inside. Her breasts jiggled and swayed. And I want to be inside you so badly it aches!"

"Oh, Kirk! I'm sorry. Let me—"

Kirk's hand on her pussy prevented her from moving, though. "Not now, sweetheart. Just lay here for a few more minutes and let me savor the moment."

"Maybe I will be the one doing the tying up tonight."

"God, woman, you're killing me here!"

Chapter Ten

Backstage for a fashion show, no matter what day it was scheduled for, was usually a madhouse. The fact that it was Valentine's Day, along with all the hype regarding the new lower-priced gowns, was netting them a lot of publicity. The excitement seemed electric and Kirk found Vicky sitting on a box in a quiet corner, with her head between her knees. She glanced up at him once and then back down.

"I can't do it."

"Of course you can do this, sweetheart. All you have to do is walk down the runway, turn around and come back." Stroking his hand over her hair, he tried to console her. "You did great in the rehearsal yesterday."

Vicky glared up at him. "I'd had two glasses of wine. I was relaxed."

"No, you didn't have that much. I was watching you."

"Nosy! Busy body!" she accused, but there wasn't any malice in her tone. "I just wish Nick wasn't playing the damned groom for the finale."

"It's all fake, Vicky. You are only saying some words in front of an actor playing the minister. In less than five minutes it will be all over and then we're off to the reception."

Vicky stared up at Kirk. How could she tell him that she wished it wasn't a fake and that he was the groom? Would he run for the hills? Slowly she sat up straight. For the last seven days, Kirk had given her a present every day, and always at a different time. Neither of them had spoken the "L" word yet, but she was in love with him. There were no more doubts in her mind.

She remembered the morning, one week ago, that Kirk had rushed off to work, leaving her alone in his bed. Rolling over, she'd felt paper crumple beneath her. Shifting about, she found a pink envelope. Her name was written on it and her first thought was that it might be a Valentine's Day card. Her fingers felt around first and noticed the bump inside. Quickly she tore open the envelope. There was not a card, but a small, bright red enameled heart fell out when she shook the envelope. It was a small lapel pin. Immediately after her shower she put it on and wore it to the office.

The next day she'd met Kirk for lunch at a trendy restaurant close to work. Since he'd made reservations, they had a nice booth and sat side by side. Taking a sip of the ice water while Kirk ordered a beer, she anxiously waited for him to turn her way. Her words spilled out once he did.

"I'm screwed."

Kirk's grin was instantaneous. "I thought that was my job."

"Eek!" she screeched a second later as his hand came up her thigh.

"Naughty girl! You've got on stockings." Kirk lightly slid his fingers along the top edge of the nylons, slipping under the lace and elastic garter. Hearing him call her "naughty" made her feel hot and tingly, especially in the spot where his hand seemed intent on reaching.

"I shouldn't have worn a skirt," she said lamely while she tried to focus on something, anything, other than the pursuit of his hand.

"I'm not complaining," he assured her. "Now why are you screwed?"

"I ran out of excuses to avoid meeting our parents for dinner."

Kirk shrugged. "I'll call Dad and tell him I canceled my plans and I'll join them after all." He paused and took a sip of the beer the waiter had just delivered.

"It gets worse." Vicky shook her head while she spread her thighs to allow his hand to slide between them, and hopefully higher. "My mother wants to fix me up on a date."

Kirk's hand stopped immediately. "With who?"

"She didn't say. I was hoping you could help me come up with some kind of good excuse to get out of it." All she wanted was to spend her evenings and nights with Kirk. "I enjoy going to dinner with your dad and my mom, but I know I'd slip up in front of them."

"What are you planning on wearing tonight?" Kirk asked.

For a moment, she was a little perturbed that he wasn't more upset, or that he wasn't insisting they tell their parents. He appeared to be accepting the fact she might be going on a date with another man almost laconically. Logically, she told herself, I could tell them. But she didn't want to ruin things between them, or their parents. Shrugging, she answered him. "That high-necked black dress."

"Good choice. Where are you going?"

"I don't know yet. Mom didn't say."

Kirk leaned closer and kissed her cheek. "I'll find out and drop in a few minutes after you arrive." His hand slipped up a little higher. "What the hell?"

Vicky grinned at his expression. "Surprise! I took my panties off before we left work."

"I'm going to start renting hotel rooms for lunch instead of reserving tables at good restaurants."

Vicky made a low purring noise in her throat. "I wouldn't object to that idea. Order us room service at the same time. Then you could properly take care of your naughty girl." She giggled her way through most of the lunch.

He'd had her scoot away on the bench when they were done eating and then lifted her left foot. His fingers lightly moving over her skin soon had the usual sensual shivers shooting through her body. It took her a moment to realize what he was doing.

The previous night in bed, he had removed her ankle bracelet under the excuse of massaging lotion into her skin after a shower. She'd actually forgotten that she had not put it back on until now. Kirk must have found the anklet and brought it along. "Okay, done," he announced, sliding off his seat, having already paid the bill. He held his hand out to her.

Taking a deep breath to calm her aroused senses, Vicky slid to the edge of the booth bench as well. She lifted her leg to glance at her anklet and stopped. This one looked the same, except as she twisted her ankle she saw the small golden heart woven in the links. Quickly she told herself not to read too much into this gift. A heart was a decorative item in lots of different jewelry, and the fact it was six days before Valentine's Day was probably a fluke.

She'd kissed his cheek circumspectly, but whispered in his ear. "Thank you. Tonight I'll show you how nice my present is."

* * * * *

"Vicky!"

Hearing Denise yelling her name returned her to the present, Kirk and the imminent fashion show. As Denise ran toward them, Vicky didn't need to ask what the other woman wanted. Most likely her mother had given her former secretary the job of keeping an eye on her daughter for the duration of the show.

"No more running, sweetheart," Kirk murmured as his new personal assistant stopped a few feet away.

"Come on, Vicky. I've got some paper sacks for you to blow into. We're all set!"

"No reprieve, honey." Kirk smiled as he reminded her. "I'll make sure and wave so you can focus on me. Just look right at me and everything will be fine."

Vicky looked back over her shoulder at Kirk as Denise dragged her away. Staring at Kirk during the show would help, unless he looked horrified when he saw her in a wedding dress. So far Kirk had been filling her life with joy and love. What if he suddenly changed? What if seeing her in the "commitment" dress caused him to turn tail and run?

Combining the nervousness she felt over leaving Kirk plus her feelings for him, she was confused whether the little gifts he gave her really meant something or had they just been the kind of things a wealthy man gave to the woman he was—

Her mind stumbled over the possible truth. Perhaps she was his "mistress" and all he was doing was pampering her. NO! She was not doing any more of this crazy talk. Tonight, after the show, she resolved to settle their relationship, if that's what this was. What better night than Valentine's to bring it to a climax, just not in bed? After all, she had a train to catch back home tonight.

* * * * *

Kirk returned to his office. He changed into a new, expensive suit he'd purchased for today. The tie was the palest of pinks, which the designer had insisted was the perfect — no, the only — choice for a situation like this. Shaking his head, he combed his hair. He probably should have gotten the haircut last week instead of yesterday. Now he looked like the kid who'd just come from the barbershop. Frustrated, he turned away from the mirror.

Knock. Knock.

Kirk looked over his shoulder as he called out, "Come in."

"Hello, son. Wow! Don't you look dapper! Val will probably see you and say I should have gotten a new suit."

"You have so many suits, Dad, I'm sure she can't remember which ones you've worn before. All you need is a new tie." Reaching into the shopping bag, he tossed his father a small box.

Grinning, Mark opened it. Slowly he pulled out a tie that matched Kirk's. "Are we going for the 'twin' look?"

Kirk turned from the mirror. "I need your help, Dad. All my life it's always been you and me. There was nothing that I couldn't talk over with you."

Mark had pulled his tie off and paused after putting the new one beneath the collar of his pristine white shirt. "That's something I've always admired…uhm, cherished I guess, about being your father. Is something wrong?"

"I hope you won't think so, because I need your help." Kirk watched as his father placed the tie perfectly without looking in a mirror.

"Anything, son, except robbing the bank and killing the loan officer."

Kirk laughed at his father. "Well, you know how Valentina planned to end the show today?"

"With Vicky and Ingles doing the wedding vows?"

"Yeah. I need you to help me snatch Ingles and tie him up before that."

"You want it to look like Vicky got stood up? Trust me, Kirk, that would not be a wise idea."

"I'm going to be the groom," Kirk told his father, holding his gaze.

"Does Vicky or Val know about this?" Mark paused in knotting his tie. "Nothing can upset a gal quicker than a last minute change in her wedding plans."

"I want to ask her to marry me. I figure if she's already in the dress and in front of a crowd, it will be harder for her to turn me down." Kirk watched his father's face, waiting and looking for any sign that his father had been aware of his feelings for Vicky.

Mark finished with his tie, and then lowered his hands. "Looks like Valentina's right after all. Well, I might as well let you in on her secret plans."

Kirk's eyes opened wide as his father started to speak—

* * * * *

"Stop fretting, Vicky! You only have two outfits, the two lingerie sets and then the finale."

Valentina smiled at her daughter, who was blowing into the paper bag. Everything was going perfectly so far. She reached into her pocket and pulled out a small box. "To maintain the illusion, darling, I want you to wear this."

Vicky looked at the old-style ring box and shook her head. Her "no" was muffled by the sack.

"Yes, Victoria." Without pause, Val grabbed her daughter's left hand. Quickly she flicked open the box and removed the ring. She slipped the diamond onto Vicky's ring finger. "Please, wear it for me."

"Mom!"

"Hush and keep breathing. I had it redone slightly and I want you to keep it."

"But it was Grandmother's engagement ring," Vicky said breathily, in between blowing in and out of the sack.

"Please, Vicky, no arguments. I want you to have this, and just for today wear it on that finger. It will look wonderful with those new diamond earrings you bought yourself. Now, I'll let Denise help you get ready."

* * * * *

As soon as Valentina left, Vicky lowered the sack. She stared at the ring, amazed at how pretty it was. Denise's voice distracted her.

"Why does your mother think you bought those earrings? I thought you were going to tell her two days ago, when you had lunch."

"I chickened out. She was with Mark when she first noticed them and I couldn't think of how to tell them together."

"Those were present number three, right?" Denise asked, picking up a brush to start working on Vicky's hair. After the bag-breathing woman nodded, she continued. "The roses were the next day, followed by the silly monkey with the pink pillow."

Vicky lowered the small sack. "The monkey with the big red butt. Kirk told me it is a Mandrill baboon."

Denise giggled. "It was Dave that helped him with gift number six."

"Well, tell him thank you very much, but what am I to do with a puppy? It obviously can't travel home with me on the train."

"You could stay here, Vicky. Your mother would be ecstatic if you moved back home."

"I know, but what if things don't work out—"

"Hush! Bite your tongue. I'm sure he really cares for you."

"I love him, but what if he is just…you know, sowing the wild oats?" Vicky lifted the bag and started breathing quickly in and out again.

Denise shook her head. "Stop that right now. Breathe slowly. Focus, and tell me what today's gift was."

"I got an expensive piece of chocolate. It was quite tasty," Vicky answered quickly, and then resumed breathing into the bag.

"At least it wasn't a whole box. If you're like me, I'd feel the need to eat it all so he'd know I appreciated the gift."

"Me too, and I saved the gold box."

Both women laughed and Vicky soon calmed down enough to finish her makeup and hair. There was just enough time to slip on the first outfit, which was a pretty peach-colored dress. There were comfortable shoes and purse, along with a beautiful sweater to make a casual ensemble perfect for travel, sightseeing or shopping.

On her first trip down the runway, Vicky saw Kirk standing at the back of the room. He made an elaborate show of waving his arms and she had to fight the urge to grin and laugh. Feeling much more relaxed she went back to change into the next set.

Chapter Eleven

Kirk was glad when Vicky made it all the down the runway and then back behind the side curtain without mishap. She only had two more trips before the finale and the wedding dress. He was still reeling to find out that both their parents had suspected about a relationship between their children for quite some time, but his father refused to say for just how long. Now he just had to convince her not to board the train that would take her west and away from him. It was scheduled to depart at ten. At least now she wouldn't have to face the guy chosen for her blind date—

Frowning, Kirk realized that if Valentina knew that Vicky and he were involved, why had she set her daughter up on a date with another guy in the first place? He suddenly had the distinctly unpleasant impression that his stepmother's plan was to make him jealous! Maybe Valentina's goal was to spur him to action. Well, it worked. Even if he had to follow her to the station and jump on the train with her, he wasn't letting her leave. Or at least he was determined that they define their relationship.

God! He sounded like a wimp just then. Still, wasn't that what the modern woman wanted…a man interested in commitment? Perhaps the alpha male truly was a fossil? Not that he'd ever stopped to consider it, but maybe he was one himself.

He'd always strived to be the best in school, sports and business. His father had set an excellent example of how to succeed and excel in the real world without stepping on people or trying to cheat and screw others. Besides loving him, he respected his dad. When his father had returned from the short business trip to Venice, Kirk could immediately tell something was different. Two days later he had arrived home to find his dad waiting for him. But he wasn't alone.

The first time he saw Valentina he'd been struck by her smile. Then he'd noticed the way the two of them were constantly looking at one another. By the time they got the courage up to tell him, he'd already guessed what they were going to announce. Since they were from a different generation, they didn't want to just "shack up." They planned a quick wedding.

Hell! He could still recall his anger at learning Valentina's daughter wouldn't be flying home to be with her mother. After two years, he figured she should be over her fears. Meeting her now, he understood a little better. Hopefully, they would work on getting her past the fears so they could enjoy traveling. Even his dad had suggested the four of them take a trip together.

Kirk paused as he realized that his father had made that suggestion last week. Most likely that meant he knew about his son and stepdaughter's relationship. It was doubtful he would have brought it up otherwise.

As soon as he made it through today, he and Vicky would pin their parents down and find out just how long they suspected before they knew the truth. Vicky was probably going to be as surprised as he was. He acknowledged that if the truth had come out sooner, no doubt their "alone time" would have greatly diminished.

Clapping caught his attention and he looked up. He had missed Vicky's second outfit and she was now coming down the runway in the sexy merry widow lingerie outfit, complete with a trailing veil with headpiece. He hadn't realized how sexy this whole underwear ensemble was going to be. Moving away from the wall, he waited until she began her return. He had about fifteen minutes to get in position.

* * * * *

"Keep breathing, Vicky, only one more to go. Just be glad you aren't flying."

Vicky glared at Denise. "You're being helpful," she said sarcastically, which was muffled by the sack and the breathing.

"Come on, darling." Her mother sailed around the corner. "Bring your sack because we are going out to let Henri and Jean Paul perform their magic on you. I've got the dress, shoes and veil out there already."

Vicky moaned but she stood to follow her mother. She knew this bout of hyperventilation and nerves was only partially due to the fashion show. What was bothering her most was that she was going to board a train late tonight and it was looking like Kirk was planning on letting her go. Frowning, she took a seat to have her makeup done.

Lowering the sack, she focused on breathing calmly and deeply. It was hard to acknowledge that it was partly her fault. There was no reason that she couldn't have brought the subject up. These were modern times and she was an empowered woman, right? She'd had a couple of opportunities to discuss a future between them or not.

After plenty of thinking, and stewing on her own, she knew what she wanted.

Time.

That is precisely what they needed to explore whether what they had was real and had a future, or if it was just lust. If it was only sexual heat, then things would be doomed. That seemed to be how a lot of relationships like this turned out. Still she knew how she felt…right?

Vicky focused on the face in the mirror. She'd been in a whirlwind of emotion since she'd gotten home. Before Kirk entered her life, she had definitely suffered Valentine Day burnout to the nth degree. Her past had provided the initial wounding, but she had done nothing to stop the growing cynicism. Granted, it would not have been easy, but she possibly could have turned the downward spiral around.

The last two years, with the coincidence of her ended engagement to Nick and her being in the air during the morning hours of 9/11, had been spent hardening her heart and developing a cynical shell to deal with anything romantic. She had fibbed when her mother had asked if she'd been dating since her move. She'd started buying Men's style magazine so she could create interesting men to tell her mother. By her phones she kept a list of names, careers and hobbies she could interchange to makeup her "date."

Kirk had found the way inside her barriers and she wasn't even sure how he did it, or when his campaign had started. But somehow, some way, he had slipped inside her castle walls. Her body had yielded first, and foolishly she had assumed that was all it would be. She was modern and she could be like a man, enjoy a one-night stand. Or a two-week stand?

Suddenly Henri was turning her chair away from the mirror. She closed her eyes while he worked his magic, turning her into a painted doll. Fighting a smile, she wondered if Kirk would even recognize her with all this stuff on her face. Most of their time together she'd skipped makeup completely, or just used some lipstick or blush. She'd do whatever her mother wanted, though. Since her arrival — even before — Vicky had been fighting the feelings of guilt she felt for not flying home for the wedding. She'd copped out and thought only of herself, not her mother.

Now she might be risking the very happiness of her mother's marriage. If necessary, she'd claim that she had seduced Kirk. The last thing she wanted was for her mother and Kirk's father to fight. Maybe it was convoluted thinking, but she was running out of ideas.

"Time for hair, Vicky."

Vicky stood without looking in the mirror and walked with Denise to the hair artist, Jean Paul. Again she closed her eyes, not really wanting to see herself transformed. When the snipping and clicking of scissors sounded in her ears, she reconsidered her easy capitulation. Focusing on her breathing, she blotted out all her worrisome thoughts. Deciding to copy Scarlet O'Hara, she would worry about all of this tomorrow. Or tonight, depending on what caused the biggest bombshell.

*****

"And now, ladies and gentlemen, we present the beautiful bride of Valentine's Day!"

Vicky heard the applause beginning as she stepped from behind the curtain. The facial veil was pulled back so her head was visible. Walking slowly, she saw people standing and continuing to applaud. Smiling, she was glad for her mother. This success would be quite a boon to her mother's business. For that reason alone she would go through the fake wedding with Nick. And tonight, alone on the train, she could replay it in her mind, changing the groom's face to Kirk's.

Turning at the far end of the runway, she started toward the stage. Since she was smiling, looking at the people, it took her a few seconds to realize that the stage had been changed. There was now a large heart-shaped trellis covered in roses and a small dais in front of it. In fact, it resembled a sketch she'd been fooling around with one day at her mother's worktable.

"What is that, Vicky?"

Surprised at being caught, she had tried to hide the drawing. Her mother was too quick and had pulled it from beneath her arm.

"That's lovely, sweetheart."

Vicky had watched as her mother's eyes roamed over her drawing. There was a traditional bride and groom, and behind them was a heart-shaped rose trellis. "I was just fooling around, trying out ideas for next season's greeting cards."

"I love the roses, Vicky."

Her mother had not said anything else, but it was obvious that she'd used Vicky's idea for the set design of this pseudo-wedding. Pushing down all of her "if-only" thoughts, she took a deep breath and continued toward the stage. The bridesmaids who'd already appeared on the runway were lined up on either side and she saw the actor who was playing the minister smiling at her. As she reached the stage, she turned toward the groom.

It wasn't Nick!

"Don't faint on us now, Vicky darling!" Kirk told her softly as he stepped forward and took her hand. "I hope you don't mind me stepping in for Nick."

Vicky felt her heart in her throat. This was better than pretending with Nick. And tonight, when she played her pretend game at the reception, Kirk was definitely the right groom. So in a way, everything was working out just fine, wasn't it?

"I know just what do, honey. I watched the rehearsal, and I'm sure I can get the lines right. All you have to say is 'I do' and marry me."

When Kirk winked Vicky had to smile. He was the man who reawakened her heart and deluged her with so many presents this last week she was starting to believe in hearts and flowers. Even though he had not yet mentioned an "ever after" for them, she could feel the little ray of hope starting to glow more brightly inside of her soul.

"Dearly beloved—"

Vicky turned her attention to the so-called minister and tried to pay attention. Kirk's voice sounded so sure and steady when he said his part.

"I take you, Victoria Lynne Vale, for my lawfully wedded wife."

Then he slipped a ring on her finger and she was amazed at her mother's planning and attention to details. Of course it was little things like this that had made her one of the most popular designers for wedding gowns in the country.

"Repeat after me, Victoria," the minister intoned in his deep, very serious sounding voice.

"I take you, Kirk Victor Magnuson, to be my lawfully—" Her voice cracked and she had to clear her it before she could go on. Her nervousness was so obvious, she thought to herself, you'd think this was the real thing, for gosh sakes! "My lawfully wedded husband."

Somehow she got through the rest of it. The minister was announcing the final lines when she caught sight of her mother standing in the wings with Mark's arm around her shoulders. It was obvious that her mother was crying, and right before Kirk kissed her she had the eeriest feeling that this was real. Kirk's kiss took her mind off her concerns.

After his lips left hers, things got very hectic. Her mother took her walk down the runway after all the models had come back out to accept the congratulations of the crowd. One of the models gave her a huge bouquet of pink roses and then the after-show soiree began in the large room next door. Many of the models were to wear the clothing and continue to circulate through the crowd, which included many interested future brides as well as the trade journalists and photographers.

Chapter Twelve

Vicky gave her ticket to the steward.

"Oh yes, Ms. Vale. Your ticket has been upgraded. You are in one of our nicest cabins. Go down to the next car. You're in cabin C."

Vicky was too tired to argue. If they figured out their mistake and kicked her out, she'd leave. There was a different train steward for this car, and he immediately relieved her of her bag and escorted her to the cabin. Opening the door, the steward began showing her around the small, but cleverly designed space.

"The dining car is open until midnight, but dinner has been ordered for you in your cabin. It will be delivered about thirty minutes after we depart. Here's your key. My name is Howard and let me know if you need anything."

"Thank you," Vicky told him, handing him a tip as he left.

She felt kind of silly actually. Her mother had insisted that she wear a traditional new-bride traveling suit, as well as accepting two new pieces of luggage.

"I insist on this little gift, darling." Valentina had hugged her daughter fiercely as Vicky left her outside the train station. "I got Denise to help me and we transferred your clothes. Mark is paying the porter to have your bags taken to the train."

"Thank you, Mom. I'll call when I get back to my apartment." Vicky brushed the tears off her cheeks. She looked around, but there was still no sign of Kirk. The party had run long, so her mother had canceled their dinner plans. She kept trying to find Kirk, but it seemed as the floor had swallowed him whole! Before she could say anything else, Mark was there, saying goodbye as well.

"As soon as Val wraps this season up, we are taking a cruise. We'll fly out to see you before we leave," Mark told her with a smile.

"Great! I'll look forward to it."

Vicky plopped down onto the sofa that would turn into a bed when she rang for the steward. She leaned her head back, closing her eyes. Soon the tears she'd managed to hold at bay began streaming down her cheeks.

At the reception, still dressed as a bride, Vicky had done her part of wandering around and so forth. Lots of people commented on how lovely the dress was and how excited they were with the line and the changes they'd seen so far. Just relieved to be done with the runway, she had lost track of time.

Kirk had appeared at her side and said he wanted to talk with her. Vicky went with him eagerly. She was sure that he was going to ask her to stay here, with him. When he spoke, she was more than surprised.

"My father said he and Val would be taking you to the train station. I guess since you are still leaving, we should say our goodbyes now."

Vicky had felt her stomach sink to the floor. Kirk was letting her leave. He was acting as if they were friends, not lovers who'd spent every day together for almost two weeks. Knowing that she had to speak, she had forced some words out.

"All right. I…uhm, I guess so."

Silence had followed her words and she knew that technically he'd said goodbye, so it was her turn to say hers. But there was no way she could say it. Every part of her had been screaming to shout, "I love you" and instead, she had to say so long, see you, and it's been great fun. This wasn't right. Swallowing hard, she had forced her next words past her constricted throat.

"I'll send for the dog."

The instant the words were out she saw the slight flare of surprise cross his face. For a moment she had considered that he had waited for her to change her mind and tell him that she'd decided to stay. But she had not done it. Instead she muttered goodbye and then ran away.

Now, sitting alone, she knew that she'd been a coward when it mattered most. All she had to do was tell him…what? Her logical side interrupted. What could she have said? I love you, Kirk, marry me? Or maybe something along the lines of "it was great shacking up, so let's keep it up."

Beneath her she felt the train begin moving. She knew that it was too late now. The time had slipped through her fingers. If she decided to move back home, her mother would insist she live with them. Sharing an apartment was okay as a temporary measure, but Vicky knew that her mother would definitely frown on her daughter living with a man and not even be engaged to him. Damn!

She kicked her shoes off and decided to get ready for bed. The steward wouldn't be back with dinner for at least ten minutes or so, and once she finished eating, hopefully she could go straight to sleep. She was certainly tired enough. Lifting one of the suitcases, she opened it. Placed on top of the other clothing she saw something wrapped in tissue paper. Peeling the thin paper aside, she saw the beautiful negligee set that she'd modeled in the show. It was the palest of pink satin and lace, shimmering like iridescent pearl. Knowing the price it would be sold for, she hesitated putting it on again. But then common sense and tiredness won.

The knock on her door came just as she was closing the suitcase. "Come in!" Looking over her shoulder, she smiled at the steward. "I'm not sure where things go, so I will let you do what you need to do and I'll step into this miniscule bathroom to be out of your way."

She had to close the door, so she listened to the sounds of things being moved and clicked. A few minutes passed and then she heard the steward call that he was done. Before she could come back out the cabin door had been closed and the lights turned out. Frustrated, she tried to remember where the lights were. Being conservative, she'd switched the bathroom light off before she'd realized the cabin was dark.

"Damn! Good thing he left before I tipped him. Now where the devil is that light switch?" Vicky took a step forward. "Great! Just great. I'll trip over something, break a part of me that could be important and then live through the disgrace of having to re-tell the story."

She froze a second later as she heard a noise coming from where the bed should be. Her heart raced for a moment or two, and then she reminded herself that she was alone. "Don't be ridiculous," she muttered softly, taking another step.

Light flared suddenly and she spun on one foot. She realized that she had been completely turned around. Blinking her eyes to adapt to the glowing brightness, she saw the candle on the tray of food. Gasping she retreated a step.

"Don't be afraid, Vicky. I didn't mean to scare you." The light clicked on and Kirk was stretched out on her bed.

"What are you doing here?" Vicky pressed her hand to her chest, as if the pressure could slow her madly racing heart.

Kirk sat up on the edge of the bed. Leaning over, he blew out the candle. "It doesn't look like my surprise is going too well, does it?" As he straightened up, his eyes moved over her body. "You look more beautiful in that nightgown than you did earlier."

Vicky shook her head. Obviously their earlier goodbye had not been the real one Kirk had planned. "It's a negligee, and I can't be more beautiful because I don't have any makeup on this time."

Kirk came to his feet, shaking his head in disagreement. "I like you better without makeup. Your lips are much sweeter when they aren't disguised by lipstick."

"With that viewpoint, the makeup industry would be out of business. But that doesn't explain why you are here, or how you said goodbye earlier."

Kirk nodded his head. "True. I have no good excuses except that suddenly I was tongue-tied. How could I say farewell when I had no intention of letting you go?"

Vicky put her hands on her hips. "But you did let me go." She stamped her foot to emphasize her point.

"You are on the train, sweetheart, that's all. I'm here with you."

"Yes, but I am on my way home," Vicky protested, and even to her ears, her voice sounded weak.

"I'm going with you to help you pack your stuff up and return back here."

"That sounds awfully high-handed," she pointed out. Then her stomach rumbled. "I need to eat."

Kirk stepped aside and gestured to the bed. "Have a seat and I'll get changed as well while you start eating."

Vicky considered protesting but decided it was useless. Kirk was here, and that was precisely where she wanted him to be. His intentions could be sorted out later. She sat on the bed, eyeing the tray of food.

"Don't wait for me, Vicky." Kirk picked up her other suitcase. He just grinned when he saw Vicky's glance. Shrugging his shoulders, he added, "They were in on this with me."

Vicky picked up the small cherry tomato from the salad she uncovered. This was almost too much to take in, she thought, eating the red fruit in one bite. Her mother had known about them, but for how long? Shaking her head in disbelief, she noticed for the first time the wine that had been poured. Picking up one glass, she drank it.

"Slow down, honey! Or at least, wait for me."

Kirk had come out of the bathroom, wearing a beautiful silky robe. She could see his bare chest, and taking a deep breath, she let her attraction for him sweep through her. Her feelings for him had not changed, that much was sure.

"Good timing then," Vicky told him with a defiant toss of her head. She wasn't giving in without some explanations, and maybe an apology. "I was going to drink yours as well."

"You could, darling. We still have the champagne to enjoy." Kirk gestured toward the door, where an ice bucket contained a bottle.

"Are we celebrating something?" Vicky asked while she began lifting the lids off the different foods. "This smells great!"

Kirk sat beside her on the bed and accepted the plate she passed him a few seconds later. "Eat first, talk later?"

Vicky shook her head, chewing a bite of the delicious roast beef. "Taste that," she said even as she filled her fork with the whipped potatoes.

"Yes, it's very good. But you haven't said if you agree or not."

Vicky nodded, reaching for the small silver gravy boat. She added more to her plate and then offered to pour for Kirk. He accepted, but prodded her again for an answer.

"Well?"

Vicky gestured that her mouth was full and she kept it that way until her plate was empty. Setting it down, she patted her stomach. "Whew! I'm full. Is there dessert?"

Kirk moved quickly. In less than five seconds, Vicky was lying on her back and he was next to her. Hampered by the long negligee and robe, she didn't resist. She mollified her conscience by reminding herself that she didn't want to harm the delicate fabric.

"Dessert comes later."

Vicky fought the smile that wanted to curve her lips at Kirk's irritated tone. "What about some champagne?"

"Answer me first."

"You didn't ask a question," Vicky pointed out with a patient tone.

"Yes I did. I asked you to move back to New York."

Vicky looked at his face. She could argue about it, or even make him explain it to her. But she saw in his eyes the look she'd seen on his father's face when he gazed at her mother. He had not told her that he loved her, or was in love with her, but as long as he continued to look at her that same way, she'd be happy.

"Okay," she whispered softly. Immediately, she knew that she had shocked him by the changed look on his face. Lifting her hand, she curved it to the side of his face and caressed him gently. "It wouldn't be fair to Chanel to move across the country."

"Chanel! You can't call a male dog that! He won't be able to hold his head up in the park. All the other guys will make fun of him," Kirk protested, frowning.

She knew his focus on the puppy would diminish in a bit and they would discuss the finer points about moving and so on. She shifted her fingers to lightly caress over his lips. "That's silly, and besides, he's my dog."

"He needs a good 'dog' name," Kirk told her, seemingly unaware of her hand moving slowly down the side of his neck and onto his chest. "Spot, Rover or even something like Charlie."

Vicky used both hands to push Kirk's robe back off his shoulders. "I think we'll have to get another puppy. A girl for me. They'll be company for each other. That way when you take Spike, or whatever his name may be, for a walk, I'll have my little Coco with me."

Kirk grinned and shrugged his robed off. His hand moved from her waist upward to cup her breast. He squeezed when her back arched and pressed more fully into his grasp. "I like that idea. I can just see us walking the dogs with our pooper scoopers."

"Do you think our parents will babysit?" Vicky sighed as Kirk's fingers began to caress and tease her nipple.

"I'm sure they'll jump at the opportunity. Especially since we won't be asking my dad to walk a male dog he has to call Chanel."

"You don't think he'd be willing to do that out of love for his son?"

Kirk pressed the softest of kisses to her lips. "Maybe, but I know for sure he'd do it because he loves his stepdaughter, and soon to be daughter-in-law."

Vicky felt her heart catch, as did her breath, at his words. She could barely breathe. Daughter-in-law? "You want to get married."

"Of course I want to marry you, only this time for real. I love you."

Vicky flung her arms around his neck, hugging him close. She told herself to slow down—

Kirk pulled her arms down and then reached into the pocket of his robe. Giving the object a shake, he held the small paper bag up to Vicky's face. He grinned at her as she took it, continuing to breathe in and out.

"Thanks," she told him, which sounded muffled inside the sack. "I love…you…too!"

"Val packed me a handful."

"Not…very…romantic!"

Kirk shook his head and sat up slowly. "I wouldn't say that, honey. Besides, I at least had you in the right position."

"How long...do we have?" Vicky asked surprised at how quickly it was going away.

"We have all night and the next couple of days—"

Vicky lowered the bag. "That's not what I meant. I was wondering when you have to be back to work."

Kirk pushed the bag back up to cover her mouth again. "Keep going. We have two weeks, but I'm sure my dad will happily help Val if we need a little more time."

Vicky continued to breathe in and out of the bag. Her voice was slightly muffled as she questioned him. "Who's watching Chanel if you are here?"

"Keep breathing, sweetheart. Denise and Dave have him until we get back."

Vicky nodded and then she tossed the bag aside. Smiling up at him, she used her eager fingers to untie his robe. "Now, why don't you show me the other way you know to increase my respirations? No paper bags required."

Kirk obeyed Vicky, making sure that she was completely satisfied with his demonstration.

About the author:

Mlyn is a Midwest gal, living all her life to date in the same house, and for the last 13 years with Georgia, a feline potentate. She worked as a Pediatrics nurse for 23 years, and began writing regularly in 1997 for her website, smoothtales.com. Her first story was electronically published by Ellora's Cave in 2002. She also enjoys crafting and has another web site where she displays her art, mlynsart.com. Her email is mlynhurn@insightbb.com, and she replies to all who write. Mlyn enjoys hearing both good and bad comments on her writings.

Mlyn welcomes mail from readers. You can write to her c/o Ellora's Cave Publishing at 1056 Home Ave. Akron, Oh 44310-3502.

Also by Mlyn Hurn:

Blood Dreams: Blood Dreams
Blood Dreams: Endless Nights
Blood Dreams: Hunters Legacy
Burning Desires
Cattleman
Christmas in Virginia
Crown Jewels
Elemental Desires
Elemental Desires (Anthology)
Ellora's Cavemen: Tales from the Temple IV (Anthology)
Enter the Dragon (Anthology)
Family and Promises
Family Secrets
High Seas Desire
His Dance Lessons
Medieval Mischief
Passionate Hearts (Anthology)
Rebel Slave
Submissive Passion
Things That Go Bump In The Night III (Anthology)
Voyage to Submission

Enjoy this excerpt from
Shooting Stars
© Copyright Bella Andre, 2004

All Rights Reserved, Ellora's Cave Publishing, Inc.

Christina looked down at the head between her spread thighs. No doubt about it, when it came to cunnilingus Jake was certainly proficient. He was the first guy she had been out with since moving to San Francisco last week, and after a couple weeks of celibacy she had really been looking forward to some hot sex. Sex was always on her to-do list, usually somewhere around number one.

She had planned her seduction well even though she hadn't known exactly whom she was going to seduce yet, giving plenty of thought to her outfit, makeup and scent. She had walked into the Holy Cow dance club in the South of Market district of San Francisco wearing tight black jeans, a skimpy white tank top—sans bra, of course—and bright red fuck-me heels. As soon as she entered the club, she could see that anyone with a penis immediately wanted her. Her "working it" outfit had never failed her yet. Christina barely hid her grin of triumph, pleased that she was going to have her pick of men to take home and fuck senseless.

Even though she really didn't know anyone in town yet, apart from the slightly snarky high school principal at her temporary substitute teacher gig and some mousy, boring women she'd sat next to in the lunch room, she hadn't been nervous about heading out to the club alone. She wasn't the kind of woman who needed to have a big bunch of girlfriends with her all the time. On the contrary, Christina enjoyed her own company immensely. Unless she was feeling horny, of course, and wanted a hot, heavy penis between her legs.

And she had felt very horny tonight. So when she spotted the incredibly tall, dark and gorgeous man at the bar, she had immediately turned on the charm, asking him to dance, all the while pressing her breasts into his chest and shaking her hips provocatively. Thirty minutes later she was in Jake's bedroom, naked and spread beneath him.

But for some reason Christina just wasn't into it. Jake was a nice enough guy, but deep in her heart she knew he wasn't the one. It stunned her that she was thinking in terms of any guy being "the one". She wasn't looking for someone to marry her, or even love. No, she was perfectly happy with her life the way things were. Unemotional yet hot fuck-fests were just what she liked. She wasn't interested in broken hearts and declarations of love. She was only twenty-five for god's sake and had her whole life ahead of her to do all of that get-married-pump-out-the-kids-get-divorced bullshit.

She forced these depressing thoughts away and concentrated on the fact that Jake really was a master of oral sex. Blood rushed to her clit and the tips of her breasts stretched tight and hard.

Christina bit back a sigh, turning it at the last second into a groan of pleasure. Taking the sound as encouragement, Jake worked double time to please her. He sucked her swollen nub between his full lips and teased her cunt with his fingers, sliding them in and out in a rather pleasing rhythm. His free hand moved up her abdomen to caress the plump underside of her breasts. He squeezed her nipple and a dose of creamy arousal poured onto his tongue. Christina shifted her hips closer to his mouth, pushing her pussy harder against his lips and teeth.

It really was too bad that she didn't feel more strongly about Jake, she thought, as she bucked her hips into his gifted hands and mouth. After all, he used just the right pressure on her clit, just the right amount of tongue as he lapped at her, and he even slipped his fingers into her cunt at exactly the right time.

Which was, she mused, precisely the problem. She didn't want a guy who did everything just right.

Christina had always dreamt of a man who would, without a word, press her against the wall, spread her legs and fuck her long and hard. He would ignore her cries of protest, refusing to be swayed by her tears. Big and rough, yet totally committed to her every sexual desire, he would pleasure them both with his ramrod huge cock. The prison scene with Mel Gibson and Sophie Marceau in *Braveheart* played vividly in her head. Her DVD copy was almost worn out from all the times she had watched it, dildo in hand.

Why, she wondered silently as Jake's smooth cheek slid against her slick thighs, *can't modern men be more like the warriors of the past?*

Why an electronic book?

We live in the Information Age—an exciting time in the history of human civilization in which technology rules supreme and continues to progress in leaps and bounds every minute of every hour of every day. For a multitude of reasons, more and more avid literary fans are opting to purchase e-books instead of paperbacks. The question to those not yet initiated to the world of electronic reading is simply: *why?*

1. *Price.* An electronic title at Ellora's Cave Publishing and Cerridwen Press runs anywhere from 40-75% less than the cover price of the exact same title in paperback format. Why? Cold mathematics. It is less expensive to publish an e-book than it is to publish a paperback, so the savings are passed along to the consumer.
2. *Space.* Running out of room to house your paperback books? That is one worry you will never have with electronic novels. For a low one-time cost, you can purchase a handheld computer designed specifically for e-reading purposes. Many e-readers are larger than the average handheld, giving you plenty of screen room. Better yet, hundreds of titles can be stored within your new library—a single microchip. (Please note that Ellora's Cave and Cerridwen Press does not endorse any specific brands. You can check our website at www.ellorascave.com or

www.cerridwenpress.com for customer recommendations we make available to new consumers.)

3. *Mobility.* Because your new library now consists of only a microchip, your entire cache of books can be taken with you wherever you go.

4. *Personal preferences are accounted for.* Are the words you are currently reading too small? Too large? Too…**ANNOYING**? Paperback books cannot be modified according to personal preferences, but e-books can.

5. *Instant gratification.* Is it the middle of the night and all the bookstores are closed? Are you tired of waiting days—sometimes weeks—for online and offline bookstores to ship the novels you bought? Ellora's Cave Publishing sells instantaneous downloads 24 hours a day, 7 days a week, 365 days a year. Our e-book delivery system is 100% automated, meaning your order is filled as soon as you pay for it.

Those are a few of the top reasons why electronic novels are displacing paperbacks for many an avid reader. As always, Ellora's Cave and Cerridwen Press welcomes your questions and comments. We invite you to email us at service@ellorascave.com, service@cerridwenpress.com or write to us directly at: 1056 Home Ave. Akron OH 44310-3502.

Cerridwen, the Celtic Goddess of wisdom, was the muse who brought inspiration to storytellers and those in the creative arts. Cerridwen Press encompasses the best and most innovative stories in all genres of today's fiction. Visit our site and discover the newest titles by talented authors who still get inspired – much like the ancient storytellers did, once upon a time.

Cerridwen Press
www.cerridwenpress.com

*Discover for yourself why readers can't get enough of the multiple award-winning publisher
Ellora's Cave.
Whether you prefer e-books or paperbacks, be sure to visit EC on the web at
www.ellorascave.com
for an erotic reading experience that will leave you breathless.*